The Inside Of The Cup

Volume 7

Winston Churchill

The Inside Of The Cup, Vol 7.

Winston Churchill

PO Box 2211
Fairfield, IA 52556
www.1stworldlibrary.org
First Edition

LCCN: 2003099819

Softcover ISBN: 1-59540-145-8
Hardcover ISBN: 1-4218-0695-9
eBook ISBN: 1-59540-195-4

The Inside Of The Cup, Vol 7.

contributed by Ed, Tim & Rodney
in support of
1st World Library Literary Society

TABLE OF CONTENTS

Volume 7

CHAPTER XXIII

THE CHOICE

I

Pondering over Alison's note, he suddenly recalled and verified some phrases which had struck him that summer on reading Harnack's celebrated History of Dogma, and around these he framed his reply. "To act as if faith in eternal life and in the living Christ was the simplest thing in the world, or a dogma to which one has to submit, is irreligious. . .It is Christian to pray that God would give the Spirit to make us strong to overcome the feelings and the doubts of nature. . . Where this faith, obtained in this way, exists, it has always been supported by the conviction that the Man lives who brought life and immortality to light. To hold fast this faith is the goal of life, for only what we consciously strive for is in this matter our own. What we think we possess is very soon lost."

"The feelings and the doubts of nature!" The Divine Discontent, the striving against the doubt that every honest soul experiences and admits. Thus the contrast between her and these others who accepted and went their several ways was brought home to him.

He longed to talk to her, but his days were full. Yet the

very thought of her helped to bear him up as his trials, his problems accumulated; nor would he at any time have exchanged them for the former false peace which had been bought (he perceived more and more clearly) at the price of compromise.

The worst of these trials, perhaps, was a conspicuous article in a newspaper containing a garbled account of his sermon and of the sensation it had produced amongst his fashionable parishioners. He had refused to see the reporter, but he had been made out a hero, a socialistic champion of the poor. The black headlines were nauseating; and beside them, in juxtaposition, were pen portraits of himself and of Eldon Parr. There were rumours that the banker had left the church until the recalcitrant rector should be driven out of it; the usual long list of Mr. Parr's benefactions was included, and certain veiled paragraphs concerning his financial operations. Mr. Ferguson, Mr. Plimpton, Mr. Constable, did not escape, - although they, too, had refused to be interviewed . . . .

The article brought to the parish house a bevy of reporters who had to be fought off, and another batch of letters, many of them from ministers, in approval or condemnation.

His fellow-clergymen called, some to express sympathy and encouragement, more of them to voice in person indignant and horrified protests. Dr. Annesley of Calvary - a counterpart of whose rubicund face might have been found in the Council of Trent or in mediaeval fish-markets-pronounced his anathemas with his hands folded comfortably over his stomach, but eventually threw to the winds every vestige of his ecclesiastical dignity . . . .

Then there came a note from the old bishop, who was traveling. A kindly note, withal, if non-committal, - to the effect that he had received certain communications, but that his physician would not permit him to return for another ten days or so. He would then be glad to see Mr. Holder and talk with him.

What would the bishop do? Holder's relations with him had been more than friendly, but whether the bishop's views were sufficiently liberal to support him in the extreme stand he had taken he could not surmise. For it meant that the bishop, too, must enter into a conflict with the first layman of his diocese, of whose hospitality he had so often partaken, whose contributions had been on so lordly a scale. The bishop was in his seventieth year, and had hitherto successfully fought any attempt to supply him with an assistant, - coadjutor or suffragan.

At such times the fear grew upon Hodder that he might be recommended for trial, forced to abandon his fight to free the Church from the fetters that bound her: that the implacable hostility of his enemies would rob him of his opportunity.

Thus ties were broken, many hard things were said and brought to his ears. There were vacancies in the classes and guilds, absences that pained him, silences that wrung him. . . .

Of all the conversations he held, that with Mrs. Constable was perhaps the most illuminating and distressing. As on that other occasion, when he had gone to her, this visit was under the seal of confession, unknown to her husband. And Hodder had been taken aback, on seeing her enter his office, by the very tragedy in her face - the tragedy he had momentarily beheld once before. He drew up a chair for her, and when she had sat down she gazed at him some moments without speaking.

"I had to come," she said; "there are some things I feel I must ask you. For I have been very miserable since I heard you on Sunday."

He nodded gently.

"I knew that you would change your views - become broader, greater. You may remember that I predicted it."

"Yes," he said.

"I thought you would grow more liberal, less bigoted, if you will allow me to say so. But I didn't anticipate - "she hesitated, and looked up at him again.

"That I would take the extreme position I have taken," he assisted her.

"Oh, Mr. Hodder," she cried impulsively, "was it necessary to go so far? and all at once. I am here not only because I am miserable, but I am concerned on your account. You hurt me very much that day you came to me, but you made me your friend. And I wonder if you really understand the terrible, bitter feeling you have aroused, the powerful enemies you have made by speaking so - so unreservedly?"

"I was prepared for it," he answered. "Surely, Mrs. Constable, once I have arrived at what I believe to be the truth, you would not have me temporize?"

She gave him a wan smile.

"In one respect, at least, you have not changed," she told him. "I am afraid you are not the temporizing kind. But wasn't there, - mayn't there still be a way to deal with this fearful situation? You have made it very hard for us - for them. You have given them no loophole of escape. And there are many, like me, who do not wish to see your career ruined, Mr. Hodder."

"Would you prefer," he asked, "to see my soul destroyed? And your own?"

Her lips twitched.

"Isn't there any other way but that? Can't this transformation, which you say is necessary and vital, come gradually? You carried me away as I listened to you, I was not myself when I came out of the church. But I have been thinking ever since. Consider my husband, Mr. Hodder," her voice faltered. "I shall not mince matters with you - I know you will not pretend to misunderstand me. I have never seen him so upset since since that time Gertrude was married. He is in a most cruel position. I confessed to you once that Mr. Parr had made for us all the money we possess. Everett is fond of you, but if he espouses your cause, on the vestry, we shall be ruined."

Hodder was greatly moved.

"It is not my cause, Mrs. Constable," he said.

"Surely, Christianity is not so harsh and uncompromising as that! And do you quite do justice to - to some of these men? There was no one to tell them the wrongs they were committing - if they were indeed wrongs. Our civilization is far from perfect."

"The Church may have been remiss, mistaken," the rector replied. "But the Christianity she has taught, adulterated though it were, has never condoned the acts which have become commonplace in modern finance. There must have been a time, in the life of every one of these men, when they had to take that first step against which their consciences revolted, when they realized that fraud and taking advantage of the ignorant and weak were wrong. They have deliberately preferred gratification in this life to spiritual development - if indeed they believe in any future whatsoever. For 'whosoever will save his life shall lose it' is as true to-day as it ever was. They have had their choice - they still have it."

"I am to blame," she cried. "I drove my husband to it, I made him think of riches, it was I who cultivated Mr. Parr. And oh, I suppose I am justly punished. I have never been happy for one instant since that day."

He watched her, pityingly, as she wept. But presently she raised her face, wonderingly.

"You do believe in the future life after - after what you have been through?"

"I do," he answered simply.

"Yes - I am sure you do. It is that, what you are, convinces me you do. Even the remarkable and sensible explanation you gave of it when you interpreted the parable of the talents is not so powerful as the impression that you yourself believe after thinking it out for yourself - not accepting the old explanations. And then," she added, with a note as of surprise, "you are willing to sacrifice everything for it!"

"And you?" he asked. "Cannot you, too, believe to that extent?"

"Everything?" she repeated. "It would mean - poverty. No - God help me - I cannot face it. I have become too hard. I cannot do without the world. And even if I could! Oh, you cannot know what you ask Everett, my husband - I must say it, you make me tell you everything - is not free. He is little better than a slave to Eldon Parr. I hate Eldon Parr," she added, with startling inconsequence.

"If I had only known what it would lead to when I made Everett what he is! But I knew nothing of business, and I wanted money, position to satisfy my craving at the loss of - that other thing. And now I couldn't change my husband if I would. He hasn't the courage, he hasn't the vision. What there was of him, long ago, has been killed - and I killed it. He isn't - anybody, now."

She relapsed again into weeping.

"And then it might not mean only poverty - it might mean disgrace."

"Disgrace!" the rector involuntarily took up the word.

"There are some things he has done," she said in a low voice, "which he thought he was obliged to do which Eldon Parr made him do."

"But Mr. Parr, too - ?" Hodder began.

"Oh, it was to shield Eldon Parr. They could never be traced to him. And if they ever came out, it would kill my husband. Tell me," she implored, "what can I do? What shall I do? You are responsible. You have made me more bitterly unhappy than ever."

"Are you willing," he asked, after a moment, "to make the supreme renunciation? to face poverty, and perhaps disgrace, to save your soul and others?"

"And - others?"

"Yes. Your sacrifice would not, could not be in vain. Otherwise I should be merely urging on you the individualism which you once advocated with me."

"Renunciation." She pronounced the word questioningly. "Can Christianity really mean that - renunciation of the world? Must we take it in the drastic sense of the Church of the early centuries-the Church of the Martyrs?"

"Christianity demands all of us, or nothing," he replied. "But the false interpretation of renunciation of the early Church has cast its blight on Christianity even to our day. Oriental asceticism, Stoicism, Philo and other influences distorted Christ's meaning. Renunciation does not mean asceticism, retirement from the world, a denial of life. And the early Christian, since he was not a citizen, since he took the view that this mortal existence was essentially bad and kept his eyes steadfastly fixed on another, was the victim at once of false philosophies and of the literal messianic prophecies of the Jews, which were taken over with

Christianity. The earthly kingdom which was to come was to be the result of some kind of a cataclysm. Personally, I believe our Lord merely used the Messianic literature as a convenient framework for his spiritual Kingdom of heaven, and that the Gospels misinterpret his meaning on this point.

"Renunciation is not the withdrawal from, the denial of life, but the fulfilment of life, the submission to the divine will and guidance in order that our work may be shown us. Renunciation is the assumption, at once, of heavenly and earthly citizenship, of responsibility for ourselves and our fellow-men. It is the realization that the other world, the inner, spiritual world, is here, now, and that the soul may dwell in it before death, while the body and mind work for the coming of what may be called the collective kingdom. Life looked upon in that way is not bad, but good, - not meaningless, but luminous."

She had listened hungrily, her eyes fixed upon his face.

"And for me?" she questioned.

"For you," he answered, leaning forward and speaking with a conviction that shook her profoundly, "if you make the sacrifice of your present unhappiness, of your misery, all will be revealed. The labour which you have shirked, which is now hidden from you, will be disclosed, you will justify your existence by taking your place as an element of the community. You will be able to say of yourself, at last, 'I am of use.'"

"You mean - social work?"

The likeness of this to Mrs. Plimpton's question struck

him. She had called it "charity." How far had they wandered in their teaching from the Revelation of the Master, since it was as new and incomprehensible to these so-called Christians as to Nicodemus himself!

"All Christian work is social, Mrs. Constable, but it is founded on love. 'Thou shaft love thy neighbour as thyself.' You hold your own soul precious, since it is the shrine of God. And for that reason you hold equally precious your neighbour's soul. Love comes first, as revelation, as imparted knowledge, as the divine gist of autonomy - self-government. And then one cannot help working, socially, at the task for which we are made by nature most efficient. And in order to discover what that task is, we must wait."

"Why did not some one tell me this, when I was young?" she asked - not speaking to him. "It seems so simple."

"It is simple. The difficult thing is to put it into practice - the most difficult thing in the world. Both courage and faith are required, faith that is content to trust as to the nature of the reward. It is the wisdom of foolishness. Have you the courage?"

She pressed her hands together.

"Alone - perhaps I should have. I don't know. But my husband! I was able to influence him to his destruction, and now I am powerless. Darkness has closed around me. He would not - he will not listen to me."

"You have tried?"

"I have attempted to talk to him, but the whole of my

life contradicts my words. He cannot see me except as, the woman who drove him into making money. Sometimes I think he hates me."

Hodder recalled, as his eyes rested on her compassionately, the sufferings of that other woman in Dalton Street.

"Would you have me desert him - after all these years?" she whispered. "I often think he would be happier, even now."

"I would have you do nothing save that which God himself will reveal to you. Go home, go into the church and pray - pray for knowledge. I think you will find that you are held responsible for your husband. Pray that that which you have broken, you may mend again."

"Do you think there is a chance?"

Hodder made a gesture.

"God alone can judge as to the extent of his punishments."

She got to her feet, wearily.

"I feel no hope - I feel no courage, but - I will try. I see what you mean - that my punishment is my powerlessness."

He bent his head.

"You are so strong - perhaps you can help me."

"I shall always be ready," he replied.

He escorted her down the steps to the dark blue brougham with upstanding, chestnut horses which was waiting at the curb. But Mrs. Constable turned to the footman, who held open the door.

"You may stay here awhile," she said to him, and gave Hodder her hand....

She went into the church . . . .

II

Asa Waring and his son-in-law, Phil Goodrich, had been to see Hodder on the subject of the approaching vestry meeting, and both had gone away not a little astonished and impressed by the calmness with which the rector looked forward to the conflict. Others of his parishioners, some of whom were more discreet in their expressions of sympathy, were no less surprised by his attitude; and even his theological adversaries, such as Gordon Atterbury, paid him a reluctant tribute. Thanks, perhaps, to the newspaper comments as much as to any other factor, in the minds of those of all shades of opinion in the parish the issue had crystallized into a duel between the rector and Eldon Parr. Bitterly as they resented the glare of publicity into which St. John's had been dragged, the first layman of the diocese was not beloved; and the fairer-minded of Hodder's opponents, though appalled, were forced to admit in their hearts that the methods by which Mr. Parr had made his fortune and gained his ascendency would not bear scrutiny . . . . Some of them were disturbed, indeed, by the discovery that there had come about in them, by imperceptible degrees, in the last few years a new and critical attitude towards the ways of modern finance: moat of them had an uncomfortable feeling that Hodder was somehow right, - a feeling which they sought to stifle when they reflected upon the consequences of facing it. For this would mean a disagreeable shaking up of their own lives. Few of them were in a position whence they might cast stones at Eldon Parr . . . .

What these did not grasp was the fact that that which

they felt stirring within them was the new and spiritual product of the dawning twentieth century - the Social Conscience. They wished heartily that the new rector who had developed this disquieting personality would peacefully resign and leave them to the former, even tenor of their lives. They did not for one moment doubt the outcome of his struggle with Eldon Parr. The great banker was known to be relentless, his name was synonymous with victory. And yet, paradoxically, Hodder compelled their inner sympathy and admiration! . . .

Some of them, who did not attempt peremptorily to choke the a processes made the startling discovery that they were not, after all, so shocked by his doctrines as they had at first supposed. The trouble was that they could not continue to listen to him, as formerly, with comfort.... One thing was certain, that they had never expected to look forward to a vestry meeting with such breathless interest and anxiety. This clergyman had suddenly accomplished the surprising feat of reviving the Church as a burning, vital factor in the life of the community! He had discerned her enemy, and defied his power . . . .

As for Hodder, so absorbed had he been by his experiences, so wrung by the human contacts, the personal problems which he had sought to enter, that he had actually given no thought to the battle before him until the autumn afternoon, heavy with smoke, had settled down into darkness. The weather was damp and cold, and he sat musing on the ordeal now abruptly confronting him before his study fire when he heard a step behind him. He turned to recognize, by the glow of the embers, the heavy figure of Nelson Langmaid.

"I hope I'm not disturbing you, Hodder," he said. "The janitor said you were in, and your door is open."

"Not at all," replied the rector, rising. As he stood for a moment facing the lawyer, the thought of their friendship, and how it had begun in the little rectory overlooking the lake at Bremerton, was uppermost in his mind, - yes, and the memory of many friendly, literary discussions in the same room where they now stood, of pleasant dinners at Langmaid's house in the West End, when the two of them had often sat talking until late into the nights.

"I must seem very inhospitable," said Hodder. "I'll light the lamp - it's pleasanter than the electric light."

The added illumination at first revealed the lawyer in his familiar aspect, the broad shoulders, the big, reddish beard, the dome-like head, - the generous person that seemed to radiate scholarly benignity, peace, and good-will. But almost instantly the rector became aware of a new and troubled, puzzled glance from behind the round spectacles. . ."

"I thought I'd drop in a moment on my way up town - " he began. And the note of uncertainty in his voice, too, was new. Hodder drew towards the fire the big chair in which it had been Langmaid's wont to sit, and perhaps it was the sight of this operation that loosed the lawyer's tongue.

"Confound it, Hodder!" he exclaimed, "I like you - I always have liked you. And you've got a hundred times the ability of the average clergyman. Why in the world did you have to go and make all this trouble?"

By so characteristic a remark Hodder was both amused and moved. It revealed so perfectly the point of view and predicament of the lawyer, and it was also an expression of an affection which the rector cordially, returned . . . . Before answering, he placed his visitor in the chair, and the deliberation of the act was a revelation of the unconscious poise of the clergyman. The spectacle of this self-command on the brink of such a crucial event as the vestry meeting had taken Langmaid aback more than he cared to show. He had lost the old sense of comradeship, of easy equality; and he had the odd feeling of dealing with a new man, at once familiar and unfamiliar, who had somehow lifted himself out of the everyday element in which they heretofore had met. The clergyman had contrived to step out of his, Langmaid's, experience: had actually set him - who all his life had known no difficulty in dealing with men - to groping for a medium of communication . . . .

Hodder sat down on the other side of the fireplace. He, too, seemed to be striving for a common footing.

"It was a question of proclaiming the truth when at last I came to see it, Langmaid. I could not help doing what I did. Matters of policy, of a false consideration for individuals could not enter into it. If this were not so, I should gladly admit that you had a just grievance, a peculiar right to demand why I had not remained the strictly orthodox person whom you induced to come here. You had every reason to congratulate yourself that you were getting what you doubtless would call a safe man."

"I'll admit I had a twinge of uneasiness after I came home," Langmaid confessed.

Hodder smiled at his frankness.

"But that disappeared."

"Yes, it disappeared. You seemed to suit 'em so perfectly. I'll own up, Hodder, that I was a little hurt that you did not come and talk to me just before you took the extraordinary - before you changed your opinions."

"Would it have done any good?" asked the rector, gently. "Would you have agreed with me any better than you do now? I am perfectly willing, if you wish, to discuss with you any views of mine which you may not indorse. And it would make me very happy, I assure you, if I could bring you to look upon the matter as I do."

This was a poser. And whether it were ingenuous, or had in it an element of the scriptural wisdom of the serpent, Langmaid could not have said. As a lawyer, he admired it.

"I wasn't in church, as usual, - I didn't hear the sermon," he replied. "And I never could make head or tail of theology - I always told you that. What I deplore, Hodder, is that you've contrived to make a hornets' nest out of the most peaceful and contented congregation in America. Couldn't you have managed to stick to religion instead of getting mixed up with socialism?"

"So you have been given the idea that my sermon was socialistic?" the rector said.

"Socialistic and heretical, - it seems. Of course I'm not

much of an authority on heresy, but they claim that you went out of your way to knock some of their most cherished and sacred beliefs in the head."

"But suppose I have come to the honest conclusion that in the first place these so-called cherished beliefs have no foundation in fact, and no influence on the lives of the persons who cherished them, no real connection with Christianity? What would you have me do, as a man? Continue to preach them for the sake of the lethargic peace of which you speak? leave the church paralyzed, as I found it?"

"Paralyzed! You've got the most influential people in the city."

Hodder regarded him for a while without replying.

"So has the Willesden Club," he said.

Langmaid laughed a little, uncomfortably.

"If Christianity, as one of the ancient popes is said to have remarked, were merely a profitable fable," the rector continued, "there might be something in your contention that St. John's, as a church, had reached the pinnacle of success. But let us ignore the spiritual side of this matter as non-vital, and consider it from the practical side. We have the most influential people in the city, but we have not their children. That does not promise well for the future. The children get more profit out of the country clubs. And then there is another question: is it going to continue to be profitable? Is it as profitable now as it was, say, twenty years ago?

"You've got out of my depth," said Nelson Langmaid.

"I'll try to explain. As a man of affairs, I think you will admit, if you reflect, that the return of St. John's, considering the large amount of money invested, is scarcely worth considering. And I am surprised that as astute a man as Mr. Pair has not been able to see this long ago. If we clear all the cobwebs away, what is the real function of this church as at present constituted? Why this heavy expenditure to maintain religious services for a handful of people? Is it not, when we come down to facts, an increasingly futile effort to bring the influences of religion - of superstition, if you will - to bear on the so-called lower classes in order that they may remain contented with their lot, with that station and condition in the world where - it is argued - it has pleased God to call them? If that were not so, in my opinion there are very few of the privileged classes who would invest a dollar in the Church. And the proof of it is that the moment a clergyman raises his voice to proclaim the true message of Christianity they are up in arms with the cry of socialism. They have the sense to see that their privileges are immediately threatened.

"Looking at it from the financial side, it would be cheaper for them to close up their churches. It is a mere waste of time and money, because the influence on their less fortunate brethren in a worldly sense has dwindled to nothing. Few of the poor come near their churches in these days. The profitable fable is almost played out."

Hodder had spoken without bitterness, yet his irony was by no means lost on the lawyer. Langmaid, if the truth be told, found himself for the moment in the unusual predicament of being at a loss, for the rector had put forward with more or less precision the very cynical view which he himself had been clever enough to evolve.

"Haven't they the right," he asked, somewhat lamely to demand the kind of religion they pay for?"

"Provided you don't call it religion," said the rector.

Langmaid smiled in spite of himself.

"See here, Hodder," he said, "I've always confessed frankly that I knew little or nothing about religion. I've come here this evening as your friend, without authority from anybody," he added significantly, "to see if this thing couldn't somehow be adjusted peaceably, for your sake as well as others'. Come, you must admit there's a grain of justice in the contention against you. When I went on to Bremerton to get you I had no real reason for supposing that these views would develop. I made a contract with you in all good faith."

"And I with you," answered the rector. "Perhaps you do not realize, Langmaid, what has been the chief factor in developing these views."

The lawyer was silent, from caution.

"I must be frank with you. It was the discovery that Mr. Parr and others of my chief parishioners were so far from being Christians as to indulge, while they supported the Church of Christ, in operations like that of the Consolidated Tractions Company, wronging their fellow-men and condemning them to misery and hate. And that you, as a lawyer, used your talents to make that operation possible."

"Hold on!" cried Langmaid, now plainly agitated. "You have no right - you can know nothing of that affair. You do not understand business."

"I'm afraid," replied the rector, sadly, "that I understand one side of it only too well."

"The Church has no right to meddle outside of her sphere, to dictate to politics and business."

"Her sphere," said Holder, - is the world. If she does not change the world by sending out Christians into it, she would better close her doors."

"Well, I don't intend to quarrel with you, Holder. I suppose it can't be helped that we look at these things differently, and I don't intend to enter into a defence of business. It would take too long, and it wouldn't help any." He got to his feet. "Whatever happens, it won't interfere with our personal friendship, even if you think me a highwayman and I think you a - "

"A fanatic," Holder supplied. He had risen, too, and stood, with a smile on his face, gazing at the lawyer with an odd scrutiny.

"An idealist, I was going to say," Langmaid answered, returning the smile, "I'll admit that we need them in the world. It's only when one of them gets in the gear-box . . . ."

The rector laughed. And thus they stood, facing each other.

"Langmaid," Holder asked, "don't you ever get tired and disgusted with the Juggernaut car?"

The big lawyer continued to smile, but a sheepish, almost boyish expression came over his face. He had not credited the clergyman with so much astuteness.

"Business, nowadays, is - business, Holder. The Juggernaut car claims us all. It has become-if you will permit me to continue to put my similes into slang - the modern band wagon. And we lawyers have to get on it, or fall by the wayside."

Holder stared into the fire.

"I appreciate your motive in coming here," he said, at length, "and I do you the justice of believing it was friendly, that the fact that you are, in a way, responsible for me to - to the congregation of St. John's did not enter into it. I realize that I have made matters particularly awkward for you. You have given them in me, and in good faith, something they didn't bargain for. You haven't said so, but you want me to resign. On the one hand, you don't care to see me tilting at the windmills, or, better, drawing down on my head the thunderbolts of your gods. On the other hand, you are just a little afraid for your gods. If the question in dispute were merely an academic one, I'd accommodate you at once. But I can't. I've thought it all out, and I have made up my mind that it is my clear duty to remain here and, if I am strong enough, wrest this church from the grip of Eldon Parr and the men whom he controls.

"I am speaking plainly, and I understand the situation thoroughly. You will probably tell me, as others have done, that no one has ever opposed Eldon Parr who has not been crushed. I go in with my eyes open, I am willing to be crushed, if necessary. You have come here to warn me, and I appreciate your motive. Now I am going to warn you, in all sincerity and friendship. I may be beaten, I may be driven out. But the victory will be mine nevertheless. Eldon Parr and the men who stand with him in the struggle will never recover from the blow I shall give them. I shall leave them crippled because I have the truth on my side, and the truth is irresistible. And they shall not be able to injure me permanently. And you, I regret deeply to say, will be hurt, too. I beg you, for no selfish reason, to consider again the part you intend to play in this affair."

Such was the conviction, such the unlooked-for fire with which the rector spoke that Langmaid was visibly shaken and taken aback in spite of himself.

"Do you mean," he demanded, when he had caught his breath, "that you intend to attack us publicly?"

"Is that the only punishment you can conceive of?" the rector asked. The reproach in his voice was in itself a denial.

"I beg your pardon, Hodder," said the lawyer, quickly. "And I am sure you honestly believe what you say, but - "

"In your heart you, too, believe it, Langmaid. The retribution has already begun. Nevertheless you will go on - for a while." He held out his hand, which Langmaid took mechanically. "I bear you no ill-will. I am sorry that you cannot yet see with sufficient clearness to save yourself."

Langmaid turned and picked up his hat and stick and left the room without another word. The bewildered, wistful look which had replaced the ordinarily benign and cheerful expression haunted Hodder long after the lawyer had gone. It was the look of a man who has somehow lost his consciousness of power.

CHAPTER XXIV

THE VESTRY MEETS

At nine o'clock that evening Hodder stood alone in the arched vestry room, and the sight of the heavy Gothic chairs ranged about the long table brought up memories of comfortable, genial meetings prolonged by chat and banter....The noise of feet, of subdued voices beside the coat room in the corridor, aroused him. All of the vestry would seem to have arrived at once.

He regarded them with a detached curiosity as they entered, reading them with a new insight. The trace of off-handedness in Mr. Plimpton's former cordiality was not lost upon him - an intimation that his star had set. Mr. Plimpton had seen many breaches healed - had healed many himself. But he had never been known as a champion of lost causes.

"Well, here we are, Mr. Hodder, on the stroke," he remarked. "As a vestry, I think we're entitled to the first prize for promptness. How about it, Everett?"

Everett Constable was silent.

"Good evening, Mr. Hodder," he said. He did not offer to shake hands, as Mr. Plimpton had done, but sat down at the far end of the table. He looked tired and worn; sick, the rector thought, and felt a sudden swelling of compassion for the pompous little man whose fibre was not as tough as that of these other condottieri: as Francis Ferguson's, for instance, although his soft hand and pink and white face framed in the black whiskers would seem to belie any fibre whatever.

Gordon Atterbury hemmed and hawed, - "Ah, Mr. Hodder," and seated himself beside Mr. Constable, in a chair designed to accommodate a portly bishop. Both of them started nervously as Asa Waring, holding his head high, as a man should who has kept his birthright, went directly to the rector.

"I'm glad to see you, Mr. Hodder," he said, and turning defiantly, surveyed the room. There was an awkward silence. Mr. Plimpton edged a little nearer. The decree might have gone forth for Mr. Hodder's destruction, but Asa Waring was a man whose displeasure was not to be lightly incurred.

"What's this I hear about your moving out of Hamilton Place, Mr. Waring? You'd better come up and take the Spaulding lot, in Waverley, across from us."

"I am an old man, Mr. Plimpton," Asa Waring replied. "I do not move as easily as some other people in these days."

Everett Constable produced his handkerchief and rubbed his nose violently. But Mr. Plimpton was apparently undaunted.

"I have always said," he observed, "that there was

something very fine in your sticking to that neighbourhood after your friends had gone. Here's Phil!"

Phil Goodrich looked positively belligerent, and as he took his stand on the other side of Hodder his father-in-law smiled at him grimly. Mr. Goodrich took hold of the rector's arm.

"I missed one or two meetings last spring, Mr. Hodder," he said, "but I'm going to be on hand after this. My father, I believe, never missed a vestry meeting in his life. Perhaps that was because they used to hold most of 'em at his house."

"And serve port and cigars, I'm told," Mr. Plimpton put in.

"That was an inducement, Wallis, I'll admit," answered Phil. "But there are even greater inducements now."

In view of Phil Goodrich's well-known liking for a fight, this was too pointed to admit of a reply, but Mr. Plimpton was spared the attempt by the entrance of. Nelson Langmaid. The lawyer, as he greeted them, seemed to be preoccupied, nor did he seek to relieve the tension with his customary joke. A few moments of silence followed, when Eldon Parr was seen to be standing in the doorway, surveying them.

"Good evening, gentlemen," he said coldly, and without more ado went to his customary chair, and sat down in it. Immediately followed a scraping of other chairs. There was a dominating quality about the man not to be gainsaid.

The rector called the meeting to order . . . .

During the routine business none of the little asides occurred which produce laughter. Every man in the room was aware of the intensity of Eldon Parr's animosity, and yet he betrayed it neither by voice, look, or gesture. There was something uncanny in this self-control, this sang froid with which he was wont to sit at boards waiting unmoved for the time when he should draw his net about his enemies, and strangle them without pity. It got on Langmaid's nerves - hardened as he was to it. He had seen many men in that net; some had struggled, some had taken their annihilation stoically; honest merchants, freebooters, and brigands. Most of them had gone out, with their families, into that precarious border-land of existence in which the to-morrows are ever dreaded.

Yet here, somehow, was a different case. Langmaid found himself going back to the days when his mother had taken him to church, and he could not bear to look at, Hodder. Since six o'clock that afternoon - had his companions but known it - he had passed through one of the worst periods of his existence. . . .

After the regular business had been disposed of a brief interval was allowed, for the sake of decency, to ensue. That Eldon Parr would not lead the charge in person was a foregone conclusion. Whom, then, would he put forward? For obvious reasons, not Wallis Plimpton or Langmaid, nor Francis Ferguson. Hodder found his, glance unconsciously fixed upon Everett Constable, who, moved nervously and slowly pushed back his chair. He was called upon, in this hour and in the church his father had helped to found, to make the supreme payment for the years of financial prosperity. Although a little man, with his shoulders thrown back and his head high, he generally looked impressive when he spoke, and his fine features and clear-cut English contributed to the effect. But now his face was strained, and his voice seemed to lack command as he bowed and mentioned the rector's name. Eldon Parr sat back.

"Gentlemen," Mr. Constable began, "I feel it my duty to say something this evening, something that distresses me. Like some of you who are here present, I have been on this vestry for many years, and my father was on it before me. I was brought up under Dr. Gilman, of whom I need not speak. All here, except our present rector, knew him. This church, St. John's, has been a part - a - large part - of my life. And anything that seems to touch its welfare, touches me.

"When Dr. Gilman died, after so many years of faithful service, we faced a grave problem, - that of obtaining a young man of ability, an active man who would be able to assume the responsibilities of a large and growing parish, and at the same time carry on its traditions, precious to us all; one who believed in and preached, I need scarcely add, the accepted doctrines of the Church, which we have been taught to think are sacred and necessary to salvation. And in the discovery of the Reverend Mr. Hodder, we had reason to congratulate ourselves and the parish. He was all that we had hoped for, and more. His sermons were at once a pleasure and an instruction.

"I wish to make it clear," he continued, "that in spite of the pain Mr. Hodder's words of last Sunday have given me, I respect and honour him still, and wish him every success. But, gentlemen, I think it is plain to all of you that he has changed his religious convictions. As to the causes through which that change has come about, I do not pretend to know. To say the least, the transition is a startling one, one for which some of us were totally unprepared. To speak restrainedly, it was a shock - a shock which I shall remember as long as I live.

"I need not go into the doctrinal question here, except to express my opinion that the fundamental facts of our religion were contradicted. And we have also to consider the effect of this preaching on coming generations for whom we are responsible. There are, no doubt, other fields for Mr. Hodder's usefulness. But I think it may safely be taken as a principle that this parish has the right to demand from the pulpit that orthodox teaching which suits it, and to which it has been accustomed. And I venture further to give it as my opinion - to put it mildly that others have been as disturbed and shocked as I. I have seen many, talked with many, since Sunday. For these reasons, with much sorrow and regret, I venture to suggest to the vestry that Mr. Hodder resign as our rector. And I may add what I believe to be the feeling of all present, that we have nothing but good will for him, although we think we might have been informed of what he intended to do.

"And that in requesting him to resign we are acting for his own good as well as our own, and are thus avoiding a situation which threatens to become impossible, - one which would bring serious reflection on him and calamity on the church. We already, in certain articles in the newspapers, have had an indication of the intolerable notoriety we may expect, although I hold Mr. Hodder innocent in regard to those articles. I am sure he will have the good sense to see this situation as I see it, as the majority of the parish see it."

Mr. Constable sat down, breathing hard. He had not looked at the rector during the whole of his speech, nor at Eldon Parr. There was a heavy silence, and then Philip Goodrich rose, square, clean-cut, aggressive.

"I, too, gentlemen, have had life-long association with this church," he began deliberately. "And for Mr. Hodder's sake I am going to give you a little of my personal history, because I think it typical of thousands of men of my age all over this country. It was nobody's fault, perhaps, that I was taught that the Christian religion depended on a certain series of nature miracles and a chain of historical events, and when I went East to school I had more of this same sort of instruction. I have never, perhaps, been overburdened with intellect, but the time arrived nevertheless when I began to think for myself. Some of the older boys went once, I remember, to the rector of the school - a dear old man - and frankly stated our troubles. To use a modern expression, he stood pat on everything. I do not say it was a consciously criminal act, he probably saw no way out himself. At any rate, he made us all agnostics at one stroke.

"What I learned in college of science and history and philosophy merely confirmed me in my agnosticism. As a complete system for the making of atheists and materialists, I commend the education which I received. If there is any man here who believes religion to be an essential factor in life, I ask him to think of his children or grandchildren before he comes forward to the support of Mr. Constable.

"In that sermon which he preached last Sunday, Mr. Hodder, for the first time in my life, made Christianity intelligible to me. I want him to know it. And there are other men and women in that congregation who feel as I do. Gentlemen, there is nothing I would not give to have had Christianity put before me in that simple and inspiring way when I was a boy. And in my opinion St. John's is more fortunate to-day than it ever has been in its existence. Mr. Hodder should have an unanimous testimonial of appreciation from this vestry for his courage. And if the vote requesting him to resign prevails, I venture to predict that there is not a man on this vestry who will not live to regret it."

Phil Goodrich glared at Eldon Parr, who remained unmoved.

"Permit me to add," he said, "that this controversy, in other respects than doctrine, is more befitting to the Middle Ages than to the twentieth century, when this Church and other denominations are passing resolutions in their national conventions with a view to unity and freedom of belief."

Mr. Langmaid, Mr. Plimpton, and Mr. Constable sat still. Mr. Ferguson made no move. It was Gordon Atterbury who rushed into the breach, and proved that the extremists are allies of doubtful value.

He had, apparently, not been idle since Sunday, and was armed cap-a pie with time-worn arguments that need not be set down. All of which went to show that Mr. Goodrich had not referred to the Middle Ages in vain. For Gordon Atterbury was a born school-man. But he finished by declaring, at the end of twenty minutes (much as he regretted the necessity of saying it), that Mr. Hodder's continuance as rector would mean the ruin of the church in which all present took such a pride. That the great majority of its members would never submit to what was so plainly heresy.

It was then that Mr. Plimpton gathered courage to pour oil on the waters. There was nothing, in his opinion, he remarked smilingly, in his function as peacemaker, to warrant anything but the most friendly interchange of views. He was second to none in his regard for Mr. Hodder, in his admiration for a man who had the courage of his convictions. He had not the least doubt that Mr. Hodder did not desire to remain in the parish when it was so apparent that the doctrines which he now preached were not acceptable to most of those who supported the church. And he added (with sublime magnanimity) that he wished Mr. Hodder the success which he was sure he deserved, and gave him every assurance of his friendship.

Asa Waring was about to rise, when he perceived that Hodder himself was on his feet. And the eyes of every man, save one, were fixed on him irresistibly. The rector seemed unaware of it. It was Philip Goodrich who remarked to his father-in-law, as they walked home afterwards, of the sense he had had at that moment that there were just two men in the room, - Hodder and Eldon Parr. All the rest were ciphers; all had lost, momentarily, their feelings of partisanship and were conscious only of these two intense, radiating, opposing centres of force; and no man, oddly enough, could say which was the stronger. They seemingly met on equal terms. There could not be the slightest doubt that the rector did not mean to yield, and yet they might have been puzzled if they had asked themselves how they had read the fact in his face or manner. For he betrayed neither anger nor impatience.

No more did the financier reveal his own feelings. He

still sat back in his chair, unmoved, in apparent contemplation. The posture was familiar to Langmaid.

Would he destroy, too, this clergyman? For the first time in his life, and as he looked at Hodder, the lawyer wondered. Hodder did not defend himself, made no apologies. Christianity was not a collection of doctrines, he reminded them, - but a mode of life. If anything were clear to him, it was that the present situation was not, with the majority of them, a matter of doctrines, but of unwillingness to accept the message and precept of Jesus Christ, and lead Christian lives. They had made use of the doctrines as a stalking-horse.

There was a stir at this, and Hodder paused a moment and glanced around the table. But no one interrupted.

He was fully aware of his rights, and he had no intention of resigning. To resign would be to abandon the work for which he was responsible, not to them, but to God. And he was perfectly willing - nay, eager to defend his Christianity before any ecclesiastical court, should the bishop decide that a court was necessary. The day of freedom, of a truer vision was at hand, the day of Christian unity on the vital truths, and no better proof of it could be brought forward than the change in him. In his ignorance and blindness he had hitherto permitted compromise, but he would no longer allow those who made only an outward pretence of being Christians to direct the spiritual affairs of St. John's, to say what should and what should not be preached. This was to continue to paralyze the usefulness of the church, to set at naught her mission, to alienate those who most had need of her, who hungered and thirsted after righteousness, and went away unsatisfied.

He had hardly resumed his seat when Everett Constable got up again. He remarked, somewhat unsteadily, that to prolong the controversy would be useless and painful to all concerned, and he infinitely regretted the necessity of putting his suggestion that the rector resign in the form of a resolution . . . . The vote was taken. Six men raised their hands in favour of his resignation - Nelson Langmaid among them: two, Asa Waring and Philip Goodrich, were against it. After announcing the result, Hodder rose.

"For the reason I have stated, gentlemen, I decline to resign," he said. "I stand upon my canonical rights."

Francis Ferguson arose, his voice actually trembling with anger. There is something uncanny in the passion of a man whose life has been ordered by the inexorable rules of commerce, who has been wont to decide all questions from the standpoint of dollars and cents. If one of his own wax models had suddenly become animated, the effect could not have been more startling.

In the course of this discussion, he declared, Mr. Hodder had seen fit to make grave and in his opinion unwarranted charges concerning the lives of some, if not all, of the gentlemen who sat here. It surprised him that these remarks had not been resented, but he praised a Christian forbearance on the part of his colleagues which he was unable to achieve. He had no doubt that their object had been to spare Mr. Hodder's feelings as much as possible, but Mr. Hodder had shown no disposition to spare their own. He had outraged them, Mr. Ferguson thought, - wantonly so.

He had made these preposterous and unchristian charges an excuse for his determination to remain in a position where his usefulness had ceased.

No one, unfortunately, was perfect in this life, - not even Mr. Hodder. He, Francis Ferguson, was far from claiming to be so. But he believed that this arraignment of the men who stood highest in the city for decency, law, and order, who supported the Church, who revered its doctrines, who tried to live Christian lives, who gave their time and their money freely to it and to charities, that this arraignment was an arrogant accusation and affront to be repudiated. He demanded that Mr. Hodder be definite. If he had any charges to make, let him make them here and now.

The consternation, the horror which succeeded such a stupid and unexpected tactical blunder on the part of the usually astute Mr. Ferguson were felt rather than visually discerned. The atmosphere might have been described as panicky. Asa Waring and Phil Goodrich smiled as Wallis Plimpton, after a moment's hush, scrambled to his feet, his face pale, his customary easiness and nonchalance now the result of an obvious effort. He, too, tried to smile, but swallowed instead as he remembered his property in Dalton Street . . . . Nelson Langmaid smiled, in spite of himself. . . Mr. Plimpton implored his fellow-members not to bring personalities into the debate, and he was aware all the while of the curious, pitying expression of the rector. He breathed a sigh of relief at the opening words of Hodder, who followed him.

"Gentlemen," he said, "I have no intention of being personal, even by unanimous consent. But if Mr. Ferguson will come to me after this meeting I shall have not the least objection to discussing this matter with him in so far as he himself is concerned. I can only assure you now that I have not spoken without warrant."

There was, oddly enough, no acceptance of this offer by Mr. Ferguson. Another silence ensued, broken, at last, by a voice for which they had all been unconsciously waiting; a voice which, though unemotional, cold, and matter-of-fact, was nevertheless commanding, and long accustomed to speak with an overwhelming authority. Eldon Parr did not rise.

"Mr. Hodder," he said, "in one respect seems to be under the delusion that we are still in the Middle Ages, instead of the twentieth century, since he assumes the right to meddle with the lives of his parishioners, to be the sole judge of their actions. That assumption will not, be tolerated by free men. I, for one, gentlemen, do not, propose to have a socialist for the rector of the church which I attend and support. And I maintain the privilege of an American citizen to set my own standards, within the law, and to be the sole arbitrar of those standards."

"Good!" muttered Gordon Atterbury. Langmaid moved uncomfortably.

"I shall not waste words," the financier continued. "There is in my mind no question that we are justified in demanding from our rector the Christian doctrines to which we have given our assent, and which are stated in the Creeds. That they shall be subject to the whims of the rector is beyond argument. I do not pretend to, understand either, gentlemen, the nature of the extraordinary change that has taken place in the rector of St. John's. I am not well versed m psychology. I am incapable of flights myself. One effect of this change is an attitude on which reasonable considerations would seem to have no effect.

"Our resources, fortunately, are not yet at an end. It has been my hope, on account of my former friendship with Mr. Hodder, that an ecclesiastical trial might not be necessary. It now seems inevitable. In the meantime, since Mr. Hodder has seen fit to remain in spite of our protest, I do not intend to enter this church. I was prepared, gentlemen, as some of you no doubt know, to spend a considerable sum in adding to the beauty of St. John's and to the charitable activities of the parish. Mr. Hodder has not disapproved of my gifts in the past, but owing to his present scruples concerning my worthiness, I naturally hesitate to press the matter now." Mr. Parr indulged in the semblance of a smile. "I fear that he must take the responsibility of delaying this benefit, with the other responsibilities he has assumed."

His voice changed. It became sharper.

"In short, I propose to withhold all contributions for whatever purpose from this church while Mr. Hodder is rector, and I advise those of you who have voted for his resignation to do the same. In the meantime, I shall give my money to Calvary, and attend its services. And I shall offer further a resolution - which I am informed is within our right - to discontinue Mr. Hodder's salary."

There was that in the unparalleled audacity of Eldon Parr that compelled Hodder's unwilling admiration. He sat gazing at the financier during this speech, speculating curiously on the inner consciousness of the man who could utter it. Was it possible that he had no sense of guilt? Even so, he had shown a remarkable astuteness in relying on the conviction that he (Hodder) would not betray what he knew.

He was suddenly aware that Asa Waring was standing beside him.

"Gentlemen," said Mr. Waring, "I have listened to this discussion as long as I can bear it with patience. Had I been told of it, I should have thought it incredible that the methods of the money changers should be applied to the direction and control of the house of God. In my opinion there is but one word which is suitable for what has passed here to-night, and the word is persecution. Perhaps I have lived too long I have lived to see honourable, upright men deprived of what was rightfully theirs, driven from their livelihood by the rapacity of those who strive to concentrate the wealth and power of the nation into their hands. I have seen this power gathering strength, stretching its arm little by little over the institutions I fought to preserve, and which I cherish over our politics, over our government, yes, and even over our courts. I have seen it poisoning the business honour in which we formerly took such a pride, I have seen it reestablishing a slavery more pernicious than that which millions died to efface. I have seen it compel a subservience which makes me ashamed, as an American, to witness."

His glance, a withering moral scorn, darted from under the grizzled eyebrows and alighted on one man after another, and none met it. Everett Constable coughed, Wallis Plimpton shifted his position, the others sat like stones. Asa Waring was giving vent at last to the pent-up feelings of many years.

"And now that power, which respects nothing, has crept into the sanctuary of the Church. Our rector recognizes it, I recognize it, - there is not a man here who, in his heart, misunderstands me. And when a man is found who has the courage to stand up against it, I honour him with all my soul, and a hope that was almost dead revives in me. For there is one force, and one force alone, able to overcome the power of which I speak, - the Spirit of Christ. And the mission of the Church is to disseminate that spirit. The Church is the champion on which we have to rely, or give up all hope of victory. The Church must train the recruits. And if the Church herself is betrayed into the hands of the enemy, the battle is lost.

"If Mr. Hodder is forced out of this church, it would be better to lock the doors. St. John's will be held up, and rightfully, to the scorn of the city. All the money in the world will not save her. Though crippled, she has survived one disgrace, when she would not give free shelter to the man who above all others expressed her true spirit, when she drove Horace Bentley from her doors after he had been deprived of the fortune which he was spending for his fellow-men. She will not survive another.

"I have no doubt Mr. Parr's motion to take from Mr. Hodder his living will go through. And still I urge him not to resign. I am not a rich man, even when such property as I have is compared to moderate fortunes of these days, but I would pay his salary willingly out of my own pocket rather than see him go . . . .

"I call the attention of the Chairman," said Eldon Parr,

after a certain interval in which no one had ventured to speak, "to the motion before the vestry relating to the discontinuance of Mr. Hodder's salary."

It was then that the unexpected happened. Gordon Atterbury redeemed himself. His respect for Mr. Waring, he said, made him hesitate to take issue with him.

He could speak for himself and for a number of people in the congregation when he reiterated his opinion that they were honestly shocked at what Mr. Hodder had preached, and that this was his sole motive in requesting Mr. Hodder to resign. He thought, under the circumstances, that this was a matter which might safely be left with the bishop. He would not vote to deprive Mr. Hodder of his salary.

The motion was carried by a vote of five to three. For Eldon Parr well knew that his will needed no reenforcement by argument. And this much was to be said for him, that after he had entered a battle he never hesitated, never under any circumstances reconsidered the probable effect of his course.

As for the others, those who had supported him, they were cast in a less heroic mould. Even Francis Ferguson. As between the devil and the deep sea, he was compelled, with as good a grace as possible, to choose the devil. He was utterly unable to contemplate the disaster which might ensue if certain financial ties, which were thicker than cables, were snapped. But his affection for the devil was not increased by thus being led into a charge from which he would willingly have drawn back. Asa Waring might mean nothing to Eldon Parr, but he meant a great deal to Francis Ferguson, who had by no means forgotten his sensations of satisfaction when Mrs. Waring had made her first call in Park Street on Francis Ferguson's wife. He left the room in such a state of absent-mindedness as actually to pass Mr. Parr in the corridor without speaking to him.

The case of Wallis Plimpton was even worse. He had married the Gores, but he had sought to bind himself with hoops of steel to the Warings. He had always secretly admired that old Roman quality (which the Goodriches - their connections - shared) of holding fast to their course unmindful and rather scornful of influence which swayed their neighbours. The clan was sufficient unto itself, satisfied with a moderate prosperity and a continually increasing number of descendants. The name was unstained. Such are the strange incongruities in the hearts of men, that few realized the extent to which Wallis Plimpton had partaken of the general hero-worship of Phil Goodrich. He had assiduously cultivated his regard, at times discreetly boasted of it, and yet had never been sure of it. And now fate, in the form of his master, Eldon Parr had ironically compelled him at one stroke to undo the work of years. As soon as the meeting broke up, he crossed the room.

"I can't tell you how much I regret this, Phil, he said. "Charlotte has very strong convictions, you know, and so have I. You can understand, I am sure, how certain articles of belief might be necessary to one person, and not to another."

"Yes," said Phil, "I can understand. We needn't mention the articles, Wallis." And he turned his back.

He never knew the pain he inflicted. Wallis Plimpton looked at the rector, who stood talking to Mr. Waring, and for the first time in his life recoiled from an overture.

Something in the faces of both men warned him away.

Even Everett Constable, as they went home in the cars together, was brief with him, and passed no comments when Mr. Plimpton recovered sufficiently to elaborate on the justification of their act, and upon the extraordinary stand taken by Phil Goodrich and Mr. Waring.

"They might have told us what they were going to do."

Everett Constable eyed him.

"Would it have made any difference, Plimpton?" he demanded.

After that they rode in silence, until they came to a certain West End corner, where they both descended. Little Mr. Constable's sensations were, if anything, less enviable, and he had not Mr. Plimpton's recuperative powers. He had sold that night, for a mess of pottage, the friendship and respect of three generations. And he had fought, for pay, against his own people.

And lastly, there was Langmaid, whose feelings almost defy analysis. He chose to walk through the still night the four miles - that separated him from his home. And he went back over the years of his life until he found, in the rubbish of the past, a forgotten and tarnished jewel. The discovery pained him. For that jewel was the ideal he had carried away, as a youth, from the old law school at the bottom of Hamilton Place, - a gift from no less a man than the great lawyer and public-spirited citizen, Judge Henry Goodrich - Philip Goodrich's grandfather, whose seated statue marked the entrance of the library. He, Nelson Langmaid, - had gone forth from that school resolved to follow in the footsteps of that man, - but somehow he missed the path. Somehow the jewel had lost its fire. There had come a tempting offer, and a struggle - just one: a readjustment on the plea that the world had changed since the days of Judge Goodrich, whose uncompromising figure had begun to fade: an exciting discovery that he, Nelson Langmaid, possessed the gift of drawing up agreements which had the faculty of passing magically through the meshes of the Statutes. Affluence had followed, and fame, and even that high office which the Judge himself had held, the Presidency of the State Bar Association. In all that time, one remark, which he had tried to forget, had cut him to the quick. Bedloe Hubbell had said on the political platform that Langmaid got one hundred thousand dollars a year for keeping Eldon Parr out of jail.

Once he stopped in the street, his mind suddenly going back to the action of the financier at the vestry meeting.

"Confound him!" he said aloud, "he has been a fool for once. I told him not to do it."

He stood at last in the ample vestibule of his house, singling out his latch-key, when suddenly the door opened, and his daughter Helen appeared.

"Oh, dad," she cried, "why are you so-late? I've been

watching for you. I know you've let Mr. Hodder stay."

She gazed at him with widened eyes.

"Don't tell me that you've made him resign. I can't - I won't believe it."

"He isn't going to resign, Helen," Langmaid replied, in an odd voice.

"He - he refused to."

CHAPTER XXV

"RISE, CROWNED WITH LIGHT!"

I

The Church of St. John's, after a peaceful existence of so many years, had suddenly become the stage on which rapid and bewildering dramas were played: the storm-centre of chaotic forces, hitherto unperceived, drawn from the atmosphere around her. For there had been more publicity, more advertising. "The Rector of St. John's will not talk" - such had been one headline: neither would the vestry talk. And yet, despite all this secrecy, the whole story of the suspension of Hodder's salary was in print, and an editorial (which was sent to him) from a popular and sensational journal, on "tainted money," in which Hodder was held up to the public as a martyr because he refused any longer to accept for the Church ill-gotten gains from Consolidated Tractions and the like.

This had opened again the floodgates of the mails, and it seemed as though every person who had a real or fancied grievance against Eldon Parr had written him. Nor did others of his congregation escape. The press of visitors at the parish house suddenly increased once more, men and women came to pour into his ears an appalling aeries of confessions; wrongs which, like

Garvin's, had engendered bitter hatreds; woes, temptations, bewilderments. Hodder strove to keep his feet, sought wisdom to deal patiently with all, though at times he was tried to the uttermost. And he held steadfastly before his mind the great thing, that they did come. It was what he had longed for, prayed for, despaired of. He was no longer crying in the empty wilderness, but at last in touch-in natural touch with life: with life in all its sorrow, its crudity and horror. He had contrived, by the grace of God, to make the connection for his church.

That church might have been likened to a ship sailing out of the snug harbour in which she had lain so long to range herself gallantly beside those whom she had formerly beheld, with complacent cowardice, fighting her fight: young men and women, enlisted under other banners than her own, doing their part in the battle of the twentieth century for humanity. Her rector was her captain. It was he who had cut her cables, quelled, for a time at least, her mutineers; and sought to hearten those of her little crew who wavered, who shrank back appalled as they realized something of the immensity of the conflict in which her destiny was to be wrought out.

To carry on the figure, Philip Goodrich might have been deemed her first officer. He, at least, was not appalled, but grimly conscious of the greatness of the task to which they had set their hands. The sudden transformation of conservative St. John's was no more amazing than that of the son of a family which had never been without influence in the community. But that influence had always been conservative. And Phil Goodrich had hitherto taken but a listless interest in the church of his fathers. Fortune had smiled upon him, trusts had come to him unsought. He had inherited the family talent for the law, the freedom to practise when and where he chose. His love of active sport had led him into many vacations, when he tramped through marsh and thicket after game, and at five and forty there was not an ounce of superfluous flesh on his hard body. In spite of his plain speaking, an overwhelming popularity at college had followed him to his native place, and no organization, sporting or serious, was formed in the city that the question was not asked, "What does Goodrich think about it?"

His whole-souled enlistment in the cause of what was regarded as radical religion became, therefore, the subject of amazed comment in the many clubs he now neglected. The "squabble" in St. John's, as it was generally referred to, had been aired in the press, but such was the magic in a name made without conscious effort that Phil Goodrich's participation in the struggle had a palpably disarming effect: and there were not a few men who commonly spent their Sunday mornings behind plate-glass windows, surrounded by newspapers, as well as some in the athletic club (whose contests Mr. Goodrich sometimes refereed) who went to St. John's out of curiosity and who waited, afterwards, for an interview with Phil or the rector. The remark of one of these was typical of others. He had never taken much stock in religion, but if Goodrich went in for it he thought he'd go and look it over.

Scarcely a day passed that Phil did not drop in at the parish house....And he set himself, with all the vigour of an unsquandered manhood, to help Hodder to solve the multitude of new problems by which they were beset.

A free church was a magnificent ideal, but how was it to be carried on without an Eldon Parr, a Ferguson, a Constable, a Mrs. Larrabbee, or a Gore who would make up the deficit at the end of the year? Could weekly contributions, on the envelope system, be relied upon, provided the people continued to come and fill the pews of absent and outraged parishioners? The music was the most expensive in the city, although Mr. Taylor, the organist, had come to the rector and offered to cut his salary in half, and to leave that in abeyance until the finances could be adjusted. And his example had been followed by some of the high-paid men in the choir. Others had offered to sing without pay. And there were the expenses of the parish house, an alarming sum now Eldon Parr had withdrawn: the salaries of the assistants. Hodder, who had saved a certain sum in past years, would take nothing for the present . . . . Asa Waring and Phil Goodrich borrowed on their own responsibility . . .

II

Something of the overwhelming nature of the forces Hodder had summoned was visibly apparent on that first Sunday after what many had called his apostasy. Instead of the orderly, sprucely-dressed groups of people which were wont to linger in greetings before the doors of St. John's, a motley crowd thronged the pavement and streamed into the church, pressing up the aisles and invading the sacred precincts where decorous parishioners had for so many years knelt in comfort and seclusion. The familiar figure of Gordon Atterbury was nowhere to be seen, and the Atterbury pew was occupied by shop-girls in gaudy hats. Eldon Parr's pew was filled, Everett Constable's, Wallis Plimpton's; and the ushers who had hastily been mustered were awestricken and powerless. Such a resistless invasion by the hordes of the unknown might well have struck with terror some of those who hitherto had had the courage to standup loyally in the rector's support. It had a distinct flavour of revolution: contained, for some, a grim suggestion of a time when that vague, irresponsible, and restless monster, the mob, would rise in its might and brutally and inexorably take possession of all property.

Alison had met Eleanor Goodrich in Burton Street, and as the two made their way into the crowded vestibule they encountered Martha Preston, whose husband was Alison's cousin, in the act of flight.

"You're not going in!" she exclaimed.

"Of course we are."

Mrs. Preston stared at Alison in amazement.

"I didn't know you were still here," she said, irrelevantly. "I'm pretty liberal, my dear, as you know, - but this is more than I can stand. Look at them!" She drew up her skirts as a woman brushed against her. "I believe in the poor coming to church, and all that, but this is mere vulgar curiosity, the result of all that odious advertising in the newspapers. My pew is filled with them. If I had stayed, I should have fainted. I don't know what to think of Mr. Hodder."

"Mr. Hodder is not to blame for the newspapers," replied Alison, warmly. She glanced around her at the people pushing past, her eyes shining, her colour high, and there was the ring of passion in her voice which had do Martha Preston a peculiarly disquieting effect. "I think it's splendid that they are here at all! I don't care what brought them."

Mrs. Preston stared again. She was a pretty, intelligent woman, at whose dinner table one was sure to hear the discussion of some "modern problem": she believed herself to be a socialist. Her eyes sought Eleanor Goodrich's, who stood by, alight with excitement.

"But surely you, Eleanor-you're not going in! You'll never be able to stand it, even if you find a seat. The few people we know who've come are leaving. I just saw the Allan Pendletons."

"Have you seen Phil?" Eleanor asked.

"Oh, yes, he's in there, and even he's helpless. And as I came out poor Mr. Bradley was jammed up against the wall. He seemed perfectly stunned. . . ."

At this moment they were thrust apart. Eleanor quivered as she was carried through the swinging doors into the church.

"I think you're right," she whispered to Alison, "it is splendid. There's something about it that takes hold of me, that carries one away. It makes me wonder how it can be guided - what will come of it?"

They caught sight of Phil pushing his way towards them, and his face bore the set look of belligerency which Eleanor knew so well, but he returned her smile. Alison's heart warmed towards him.

"What do you think of this?" he demanded. "Most of our respectable friends who dared to come have left in a towering rage - to institute lawsuits, probably. At tiny rate, strangers are not being made to wait until ten minutes after the service begins. That's one barbarous custom abolished."

"Strangers seem to have taken matters in their own hands for once" Eleanor smiled. "We've made up our minds to stay, Phil, even if we have to stand."

"That's the right spirit," declared her husband, glancing at Alison, who had remained silent, with approval and by no means a concealed surprise. "I think I know of a place where I can squeeze you in, near Professor Bridges and Sally, on the side aisle."

"Are George and Sally here?" Eleanor exclaimed.

"Hodder," said Phil, "is converting the heathen. You couldn't have kept George away. And it was George who made Sally stay!"

Presently they found themselves established between a rawboned young workingman who smelled strongly of soap, whose hair was plastered tightly against his forehead, and a young woman who leaned against the wall. The black in which she was dressed enhanced the whiteness and weariness of her face, and she sat gazing ahead of her, apparently unconscious of those who surrounded her, her hands tightly folded in her lap. In their immediate vicinity, indeed, might have been found all the variety of type seen in the ordinary street car. And in truth there were some who seemed scarcely to realize they were not in a public vehicle. An elaborately dressed female in front of them, whose expansive hat brushed her neighbours, made audible comments to a stout man with a red neck which was set in a crease above his low collar.

"They tell me Eldon Parr's pew has a gold plate on it. I wish I knew which it was. It ain't this one, anyway, I'll bet."

"Say, they march in in this kind of a church, don't they?" some one said behind them.

Eleanor, with her lips tightly pressed, opened her prayer book. Alison's lips were slightly parted as she gazed about her, across the aisle. Her experience of the Sunday before, deep and tense as it had been, seemed as nothing compared to this; the presence of all these people stimulated her inexpressibly, fired her; and she felt the blood pulsing through her body as she contrasted this gathering with the dignified, scattered congregation she had known. She scarcely recognized the church itself . . . She speculated on the homes from which these had come, and the motives which had brought them.

For a second the perfume of the woman in front, mingling with other less definable odours, almost sickened her, evoking suggestions of tawdry, trivial, vulgar lives, fed on sensation and excitement; but the feeling was almost immediately swept away by a renewed sense of the bigness of the thing which she beheld, - of which, indeed, she was a part. And her thoughts turned more definitely to the man who had brought it all about. Could he control it, subdue it? Here was Opportunity suddenly upon him, like a huge, curving, ponderous wave. Could he ride it? or would it crush him remorselessly?

Sensitive, alert, quickened as she was, she began to be aware of other values: of the intense spiritual hunger in the eyes of the woman in black, the yearning of barren, hopeless existences. And here and there Alison's look fell upon more prosperous individuals whose expressions proclaimed incredulity, a certain cynical amusement at the spectacle: others seemed uneasy, as having got more than they had bargained for, deliberating whether to flee . . . and then, just as her suspense was becoming almost unbearable, the service began. . .

How it had been accomplished, the thing she later felt, was beyond the range of intellectual analysis. Nor could she have told how much later, since the passage of time had gone unnoticed. Curiosities, doubts, passions, longings, antagonisms - all these seemed - as the most natural thing in the world - to have been fused into one common but ineffable emotion. Such, at least, was the impression to which Alison startlingly awoke. All the while she had been conscious of Hodder, from the moment she had heard his voice in the chancel; but somehow this consciousness of him had melted, imperceptibly, into that of the great congregation, once divided against itself, which had now achieved unity of soul.

The mystery as to how this had been effected was the more elusive when she considered the absence of all methods which might have been deemed revivalistic. Few of those around her evinced a familiarity with the historic service. And then occurred to her his explanation of personality as the medium by which all truth is revealed, by which the current of religion, the motive power in all history, is transmitted. Surely this was the explanation, if it might be called one! That tingling sense of a pervading spirit which was his, - and yet not his. He was the incandescent medium, and yet, paradoxically, gained in identity and individuality and was inseparable from the thing itself.

She could not see him. A pillar hid the chancel from her view.

The service, to which she had objected as archaic, became subordinate, spiritualized, dominated by the personality. Hodder had departed from the usual custom by giving out the page of the psalter: and the verses, the throbbing responses which arose from every corner of the church, assumed a new significance, the vision of the ancient seer revived. One verse he read resounded with prophecy.

"Thou shalt deliver me from the strivings of the people: and thou shalt make me the head of the heathen."

And the reply:

"A people whom I have not known shall serve me."

The working-man next to Alison had no prayer-book. She thrust her own into his hand, and they read from it together . . . .

When they came to the second hymn the woman in front of her had wonderfully shed her vulgarity. Her voice - a really good one - poured itself out:

"See a long race thy spacious courts adorn,
See future sons, and daughters yet unborn,
In crowding ranks on every side arise,
Demanding life, impatient for the skies."

Once Alison would have been critical of the words She was beyond that, now. What did it matter, if the essential Thing were present?

The sermon was a surprise. And those who had come for excitement, for the sensation of hearing a denunciation of a class they envied and therefore hated, and nevertheless strove to imitate, were themselves rebuked. Were not their standards the same? And if the standard were false, it followed inevitably that the life was false also.

Hodder fairly startled these out of their preconceived notions of Christianity. Let them shake out of their minds everything they had thought it to mean, churchgoing, acceptance of creed and dogma, contributive charity, withdrawal from the world, rites and ceremonies: it was none of these.

The motive in the world to-day was the acquisition of property; the motive of Christianity was absolutely and uncompromisingly opposed to this. Shock their practical sense as it might, Christianity looked forward with steadfast faith to a time when the incentive to amass property would be done away with, since it was a source of evil and a curse to mankind. If they would be Christians, let them face that. Let them enter into life, into the struggles going on around them to-day against greed, corruption, slavery, poverty, vice and crime. Let them protest, let them fight, even as Jesus Christ had fought and protested. For as sure as they sat there the day would come when they would be called to account, would be asked the question - what had they done to make the United States of America a better place to live in?

There were in the Apostolic writings and tradition misinterpretations of life which had done much harm. Early Christianity had kept its eyes fixed on another world, and had ignored this: had overlooked the fact that every man and woman was put here to do a particular work. In the first epistle of Peter the advice was given, "submit yourselves to every ordinance of man for the Lord's sake." But Christ had preached democracy, responsibility, had foreseen a millennium, the fulfilment of his Kingdom, when all men, inspired by the Spirit, would make and keep in spirit the ordinances of God.

Before they could do God's work and man's work they must first be awakened, filled with desire. Desire was power. And he prayed that some of them, on this day, would receive that desire, that power which nothing could resist. The desire which would lead each and every one to the gates of the Inner World which was limitless and eternal, filled with dazzling light . . . .

Let them have faith then. Not credulity in a vague God they could not imagine, but faith in the Spirit of the

Universe, humanity, in Jesus Christ who had been the complete human revelation of that Spirit, who had suffered and died that man might not live in ignorance of it. To doubt humanity, - such was the Great Refusal, the sin against the Holy Ghost, the repudiation of the only true God!

After a pause, he spoke simply of his hope for St. John's. If he remained here his ambition was that it would be the free temple of humanity, of Jesus Christ, supported not by a few, but by all, - each in accordance with his means. Of those who could afford nothing, nothing would be required. Perhaps this did not sound practical, nor would it be so if the transforming inspiration failed. He could only trust and try, hold up to them the vision of the Church as a community of willing workers for the Kingdom . . .

III

After the service was over the people lingered in the church, standing in the pews and aisles, as though loath to leave. The woman with the perfume and the elaborate hat was heard to utter a succinct remark.

"Say, Charlie, I guess he's all right. I never had it put like that."

The thick-necked man's reply was inaudible.

Eleanor Goodrich was silent and a little pale as she pressed close to Alison. Her imagination had been stretched, as it were, and she was still held in awe by the vastness of what she had heard and seen. Vaster even than ever, - so it appeared now, - demanding greater sacrifices than she had dreamed of. She looked back upon the old as at receding shores.

Alison, with absorbed fascination, watched the people; encountered, here and there, recognitions from men and women with whom she had once danced and dined in what now seemed a previous existence. Why had they come? and how had they received the message? She ran into a little man, a dealer in artists' supplies who once had sold her paints and brushes, who stared and bowed uncertainly. She surprised him by taking his hand.

"Did you like it?" she asked, impulsively.

"It's what I've been thinking for years, Miss Parr," he responded, "thinking and feeling. But I never knew it was Christianity. And I never thought - " he stopped and looked at her, alarmed.

"Oh," she said, "I believe in it, too - or try to."

She left him, mentally gasping . . . . Without, on the sidewalk, Eleanor Goodrich was engaged in conversation with a stockily built man, inclined to stoutness; he had a brown face and a clipped, bristly mustache. Alison paused involuntarily, and saw him start and hesitate as his clear, direct gaze met her own.

Bedloe Hubbell was one of those who had once sought to marry her. She recalled him as an amiable and aimless boy; and after she had gone East she had received with incredulity and then with amusement the news of his venture into altruistic politics. It was his efficiency she had doubted, not his sincerity. Later tidings, contemptuous and eventually irritable utterances of her own father, together with accounts in the New York newspapers of his campaign, had convinced her in spite of herself that Bedloe Hubbell had actually shaken the seats of power. And somehow, as she now took him in, he looked it.

His transformation was one of the signs, one of the mysteries of the times. The ridicule and abuse of the press, the opposition and enmity of his childhood friends, had developed the man of force she now beheld, and who came forward to greet her.

"Alison!" he exclaimed. He had changed in one sense, and not in another. Her colour deepened as the sound of his voice brought back the lapsed memories of the old intimacy. For she had been kind to him, kinder than to any other; and the news of his marriage - to a woman from the Pacific coast - had actually induced in her certain longings and regrets. When the cards had reached her, New York and the excitement of the life into which she had been weakly, if somewhat unwittingly, drawn had already begun to pall.

"I'm so glad to see you," she told him. "I've heard - so many things. And I'm very much in sympathy with what you're doing."

They crossed the street, and walked away from the church together. She had surprised him, and made him uncomfortable.

"You've been away so long," he managed to say, "perhaps you do not realize - "

"Oh, yes, I do," she interrupted. "I am on the other side, on your side. I thought of writing you, when you nearly won last autumn."

"You see it, too?" he exclaimed.

"Yes, I've changed, too. Not so much as you," she added, shyly. "I always had a certain sympathy, you know, with the Robin Hoods."

He laughed at her designation, both pleased and taken aback by her praise. . . But he wondered if she knew the extent of his criticism of her father.

"That rector is a wonderful man," he broke out, irrelevantly. "I can't get over' him - I can't quite grasp the fact that he exists, that he has dared to do what he has done."

This brought her colour back, but she faced him bravely. You think he is wonderful, then?"

"Don't you?" he demanded.

She assented. "But I am curious to know why you do. Somehow, I never thought of - you - "

"As religious," he supplied. "And you? If I remember rightly - "

"Yes," she interrupted, "I revolted, too. But Mr. Hodder puts it so - it makes one wonder."

"He has not only made me wonder," declared Bedloe Hubbell, emphatically, "I never knew what religion was until I heard this man last Sunday."

"Last Sunday!"

"Until then, I hadn't been inside of a church for fifteen years, - except to get married. My wife takes the children, occasionally, to a Presbyterian church near us."

"And why, did you go then?" she asked.

"I am a little ashamed of my motive," he confessed. "There were rumours - I don't pretend to know how they got about - " he hesitated, once more aware of delicate ground. "Wallis Plimpton said something to a man who told me. I believe I went out of sheer curiosity to hear what Hodder would have to say. And then, I had been reading, wondering whether there were anything in Christianity, after all."

"Yes?" she said, careless now as to what cause he might attribute her eagerness. "And he gave you something?"

It was then she grasped the truth that this sudden renewed intimacy was the result of the impression Hodder had left upon the minds of both.

"He gave me everything," Bedloe Hubbell replied. "I am willing to acknowledge it freely. In his explanation of the parable of the Prodigal Son, he gave me the clew to our modern times. What was for me an inextricable puzzle has become clear as day. He has made me understand, at last, the force which stirred me, which goaded me until I was fairly compelled to embark in the movement which the majority of our citizens still continue to regard as quixotic. I did not identify that force with religion, then, and when I looked back on the first crazy campaign we embarked upon, with the whole city laughing at me and at the obscure and impractical personnel we had, there were moments when it seemed incomprehensible folly. I had nothing to gain, and everything to lose by such a venture. I was lazy and easy-going, as you know. I belonged to the privileged class, I had sufficient money to live in comparative luxury all my days, I had no grudge against these men whom I had known all my life."

"But it must have had some beginning," said Alison.

"I was urged to run for the city council, by these very men." Bedloe Hubbell smiled at the recollection. "They accuse me now of having indulged once in the same practice, for which I am condemning them. Our company did accept rebates, and we sought favours from the city government. I have confessed it freely on the platform. Even during my first few months in the council what may be called the old political practices seemed natural to me. But gradually the iniquity of it all began to dawn on me, and then I couldn't rest until I had done something towards stopping it.

"At length I began to see," he continued, "that education of the masses was to be our only preserver, that we should have to sink or swim by that. I began to see, dimly, that this was true for other movements going on to-day. Now comes Hodder with what I sincerely believe is the key. He compels men like me to recognize that our movements are not merely moral, but religious. Religion, as yet unidentified, is the force behind these portentous stirrings of politics in our country, from sea to sea. He aims, not to bring the Church into politics, but to make her the feeder of these movements. Men join them to-day from all motives, but the religious is the only one to which they may safely be trusted. He has rescued the jewel from the dust-heap of tradition, and holds it up, shining, before our eyes."

Alison looked at her companion.

"That," she said, "is a very beautiful phrase."

Bedloe Hubbell smiled queerly.

"I don't know why I'm telling you all this. I can't usually talk about it. But the sight of that congregation this morning, mixed as it was, and the way he managed to weld it together."

"Ah, you noticed that!" she exclaimed sharply.

"Noticed it!"

"I know. It was a question of feeling it."

There was a silence.

"Will he succeed?" she asked presently.

"Ah," said Bedloe Hubbell, "how is it possible to predict it? The forces against him are tremendous, and it is usually the pioneer who suffers. I agree absolutely with his definition of faith, I have it. And the work he has done already can never be undone. The time is ripe, and it is something that he has men like Phil Goodrich behind him, and Mr. Waring. I'm going to enlist, and from now on I intend to get every man and woman upon whom I have any influence whatever to go to that church . . . ." A little later Alison, marvelling, left him.

CHAPTER XXVI

THE CURRENT OF LIFE

I

The year when Hodder had gone east - to Bremerton and Bar Harbor, he had read in the train a magazine article which had set fire to his imagination. It had to do with the lives of the men, the engineers who dared to deal with the wild and terrible power of the western hills, who harnessed and conquered roaring rivers, and sent the power hundreds of miles over the wilderness, by flimsy wires, to turn the wheels of industry and light the dark places of the cities. And, like all men who came into touch with elemental mysteries, they had their moments of pure ecstasy, gaining a tingling, intenser life from the contact with dynamic things; and other moments when, in their struggle for mastery, they were buffeted about, scorched, and almost overwhelmed.

In these days the remembrance of that article came back to Hodder. It was as though he, too, were seeking to deflect and guide a force - the Force of forces. He, too, was buffeted, scorched, and bruised, at periods scarce given time to recover himself in the onward rush he himself had started, and which he sought to control. Problems arose which demanded the quick thinking of emergency. He, too, had his moments of reward, the reward of the man who is in touch with reality.

He lived, from day to day, in a bewildering succession of encouragements and trials, all unprecedented. If he remained at St. John's, an entire new organization would be necessary . . . . He did not as yet see it clearly; and in the meantime, with his vestry alienated, awaiting the bishop's decision, he could make no definite plans, even if he had had the leisure. Wholesale desertions had occurred in the guilds and societies, the activities of which had almost ceased. Little Tomkinson, the second assistant, had resigned; and McCrae, who worked harder than ever before, was already marked, Hodder knew, for dismissal if he himself were defeated.

And then there was the ever present question of money. It remained to be seen whether a system of voluntary offerings were practicable. For Hodder had made some inquiries into the so-called "free churches," only to discover that there were benefactors behind them, benefactors the Christianity of whose lives was often doubtful.

One morning he received in the mail the long-expected note from the bishop, making an appointment for the next day. Hodder, as he read it over again, smiled to himself. . . He could gather nothing of the mind of the writer from the contents.

The piece of news which came to him on the same morning swept completely the contemplations of the approaching interview from his mind. Sally Grover stopped in at the parish house on her way to business.

"Kate Marcy's gone," she announced, in her abrupt fashion.

"Gone!" he exclaimed, and stared at her in dismay. "Gone where?"

"That's just it," said Miss Grover. "I wish I knew. I reckon we'd got into the habit of trusting her too much, but it seemed the only way. She wasn't in her room last night, but Ella Finley didn't find it out until this morning, and she ran over scared to death, to tell us about it."

Involuntarily the rector reached for his hat.

"I've sent out word among our friends in Dalton Street," Sally continued. An earthquake could not have disturbed her outer, matter-of-fact calmness. But Hodder was not deceived: he knew that she was as profoundly grieved and discouraged as himself. "And I've got old Gratz, the cabinet-maker, on the job. If she's in Dalton Street, he'll find her."

"But what - ?" Hodder began.

Sally threw up her hands.

"You never can tell, with that kind. But it sticks in my mind she's done something foolish."

"Foolish?"

Sally twitched, nervously.

"Somehow I don't think it's a spree - but as I say, you can't tell. She's full of impulses. You remember how she frightened us once before, when she went off and stayed all night with the woman she used to know in the flat house, when she heard she was sick?"

Hodder nodded.

"You've inquired there?"

"That woman went to the hospital, you know. She may be with another one. If she is, Gratz ought to find her. . . You know there was a time, Mr. Hodder, when I didn't have much hope that we'd pull her through. But we got hold of her through her feelings. She'd do anything for Mr. Bentley - she'd do anything for you, and the way she stuck to that embroidery was fine. I don't say she was cured, but whenever she'd feel one of those fits coming on she'd let us know about it, and we'd watch her. And I never saw one of that kind change so. Why, she must be almost as good looking now as she ever was."

"You don't think she has done anything - desperate?" asked Hodder, slowly.

Sally comprehended.

"Well - somehow I don't. She used to say if she ever got drunk again she'd never come back. But she didn't have any money she's given Mr. Bentley every cent of it. And we didn't have any warning. She was as cheerful as could be yesterday morning, Mrs. McQuillen says."

"It might not do any harm to notify the police," replied Hodder, rising. "I'll go around to headquarters now."

He was glad of the excuse for action. He could not have sat still. And as he walked rapidly across Burton Street he realized with a pang how much his heart had been set on Kate Marcy's redemption. In spite of the fact that every moment of his time during the past fortnight had been absorbed by the cares, responsibilities, and trials thrust upon him, he reproached himself for not having gone oftener to Dalton Street. And yet, if Mr. Bentley and Sally Grower had been unable to foresee and prevent this, what could he have done?

At police headquarters he got no news. The chief received him deferentially, sympathetically, took down Kate Marcy's description, went so far as to remark, sagely, that too much mustn't be expected of these women, and said he would notify the rector if she were found. The chief knew and admired Mr. Bentley, and declared he was glad to meet Mr. Hodder. . . Hodder left, too preoccupied to draw any significance from the nature of his welcome. He went at once to Mr. Bentley's.

The old gentleman was inclined to be hopeful, to take Sally Grower's view of the matter. . He trusted, he said, Sally's instinct. And Hodder came away less uneasy, not a little comforted by a communion which never failed to fortify him, to make him marvel at the calmness of that world in which his friend lived, a calmness from which no vicarious sorrow was excluded. And before Hodder left, Mr. Bentley had drawn from him some account of the more recent complexities at the church. The very pressure of his hand seemed to impart courage.

"You won't stay and have dinner with me?"

The rector regretfully declined.

"I hear the bishop has returned," said Mr. Bentley, smiling.

Hodder was surprised. He had never heard Mr. Bentley speak of the bishop. Of course he must know him.

"I have my talk with him to-morrow."

"Mr. Bentley said nothing, but pressed his hand again . . . .

On Tower Street, from the direction of the church, he beheld a young man and a young woman approaching him absorbed in conversation. Even at a distance both seemed familiar, and presently he identified the lithe and dainty figure in the blue dress as that of the daughter of his vestryman, Francis Ferguson. Presently she turned her face, alight with animation, from her companion, and recognized him.

"It's Mr. Hodder!" she exclaimed, and was suddenly overtaken with a crimson shyness. The young man seemed equally embarrassed as they stood facing the rector.

"I'm afraid you don't remember me, Mr. Hodder," he said. "I met you at Mr. Ferguson's last spring."

Then it came to him. This was the young man who had made the faux pas which had caused Mrs. Ferguson so much consternation, and who had so manfully apologized afterwards. His puzzled expression relaxed into a smile, and he took the young man's hand.

"I was going to write to you," said Nan, as she looked up at the rector from under the wide brim of her hat. "Our engagement is to be announced Wednesday."

Hodder congratulated them. There was a brief silence, when Nan said tremulously:

"We're coming to St. John's!"

"I'm very glad," Hodder replied, gravely. It was one of those compensating moments, for him, when his tribulations vanished; and the tributes of the younger generation were those to which his heart most freely responded. But the situation, in view of the attitude of Francis Ferguson, was too delicate to be dwelt upon.

"I came to hear you last Sunday, Mr. Hodder," the young man volunteered, with that mixture of awkwardness and straightforwardness which often characterize his sex and age in referring to such matters. "And I had an idea of writing you, too, to tell you how much I liked what you said. But I know you must have had many letters. You've made me think."

He flushed, but met the rector's eye. Nan stood regarding him with pride.

"You've made me think, too," she added. "And we intend to pitch in and help you, if we can be of any use."

He parted from them, wondering. And it was not until he had reached the parish house that it occurred to him that he was as yet unenlightened as to the young man's name . . . .

His second reflection brought back to his mind Kate Mercy, for it was with a portion of Nan Ferguson's generous check that her board had been paid. And he recalled the girl's hope, as she had given it to him, that he would find some one in Dalton Street to help . . . .

II

There might, to the mundane eye, have been an element of the ridiculous in the spectacle of the rector of St. John's counting his gains, since he had chosen - with every indication of insanity - to bring the pillars of his career crashing down on his own head. By no means the least, however, of the treasures flung into his lap was the tie which now bound him to the Philip Goodriches, which otherwise would never have been possible. And as he made his way thither on this particular evening, a renewed sense came upon him of his emancipation from the dreary, useless hours he had been wont to spend at other dinner tables. That existence appeared to him now as the glittering, feverish unreality of a nightmare filled with restless women and tired men who drank champagne, thus gradually achieving - by the time cigars were reached - an artificial vivacity. The caprice and superficiality of the one sex, the inability to dwell upon or even penetrate a serious subject, the blindness to what was going on around them; the materialism, the money standard of both, were nauseating in the retrospect.

How, indeed, had life once appeared so distorted to him, a professed servant of humanity, as to lead him in the name of duty into that galley?

Such was the burden of his thought when the homelike front of the Goodrich house greeted him in the darkness, its enshrouded windows gleaming with friendly light. As the door opened, the merry sound of children's laughter floated down the stairs, and it seemed to Hodder as though a curse had been lifted. . .

The lintel of this house had been marked for salvation, the scourge had passed it by: the scourge of social striving which lay like a blight on a free people.

Within, the note of gentility, of that instinctive good taste to which many greater mansions aspired in vain, was sustained. The furniture, the pictures, the walls and carpets were true expressions of the individuality of master and mistress, of the unity of the life lived together; and the rector smiled as he detected, in a corner of the hall, a sturdy but diminutive hobby-horse - here the final, harmonious touch. There was the sound of a scuffle, treble shrieks of ecstasy from above, and Eleanor Goodrich came out to welcome him.

"Its Phil," she told him in laughing despair, "he upsets all my discipline, and gets them so excited they don't go to sleep for hours..."

Seated in front of the fire in the drawing-room, he found Alison Parr. Her coolness, her radiancy, her complete acceptance of the situation, all this and more he felt from the moment he touched her hand and looked into her face. And never had she so distinctly represented to him the mysterious essence of fate. Why she should have made the fourth at this intimate gathering, and whether or not she was or had been an especial friend of Eleanor Goodrich he did not know. There was no explanation....

A bowl of superb chrysanthemums occupied the centre of the table. Eleanor lifted them off and placed them on the sideboard.

"I've got used to looking at Phil," she explained, "and

craning is so painful."

The effect at first was to increase the intensity of the intimacy. There was no reason - he told himself - why Alison's self-possession should have been disturbed; and as he glanced at her from time to time he perceived that it was not. So completely was she mistress of herself that presently he felt a certain faint resentment rising within him, - yet he asked himself why she should not have been. It was curious that his imagination would not rise, now, to a realization of that intercourse on which, at times, his fancy had dwelt with such vividness. The very interest, the eagerness with which she took part in their discussions seemed to him in the nature of an emphatic repudiation of any ties to him which might have been binding.

All this was only, on Hodder's part, to be aware of the startling discovery as to how strong his sense of possession had been, and how irrational, how unwarranted.

For he had believed himself, as regarding her, to have made the supreme renunciation of his life. And the very fact that he had not consulted, could not consult her feelings and her attitude made that renunciation no less difficult. All effort, all attempt at achievement of the only woman for whom he had ever felt the sublime harmony of desire - the harmony of the mind and the flesh - was cut off.

To be here, facing her again in such close proximity, was at once a pleasure and a torture. And gradually he found himself yielding to the pleasure, to the illusion of permanency created by her presence. And, when all was said, he had as much to be grateful for as he could reasonably have wished; yes, and more. The bond (there was a bond, after all!) which united them was unbreakable. They had forged it together. The future would take care of itself.

The range of the conversation upon which they at length embarked was a tacit acknowledgment of a relationship which now united four persons who, six months before, would have believed themselves to have had nothing in common. And it was characteristic of the new interest that it transcended the limits of the parish of St. John's, touched upon the greater affairs to which that parish - if their protest prevailed - would now be dedicated. Not that the church was at once mentioned, but subtly implied as now enlisted, - and emancipated henceforth from all ecclesiastical narrowness . . . . The amazing thing by which Hodder was suddenly struck was the naturalness with which Alison seemed to fit into the new scheme. It was as though she intended to remain there, and had abandoned all intention of returning to the life which apparently she had once permanently and definitely chosen....

Bedloe Hubbell's campaign was another topic. And Phil had observed, with the earnestness which marked his more serious statements, that it wouldn't surprise him if young Carter, Hubbell's candidate for mayor, overturned that autumn the Beatty machine.

"Oh, do you think so!" Alison exclaimed with exhilaration.

"They're frightened and out of breath," said Phil, "they had no idea that Bedloe would stick after they had licked him in three campaigns. Two years ago they tried to buy him off by offering to send him to the Senate, and Wallis Plimpton has never got through his head to this why he refused."

Plimpton's head, Eleanor declared dryly, was impervious to a certain kind of idea.

"I wonder if you know, Mr. Hodder, what an admirer Mr. Hubbell is of yours?" Alison asked. "He is most anxious to have a talk with you."

Hodder did not know.

"Well," said Phil, enthusiastically, to the rector, "that's the best tribute you've had yet. I can't say that Bedloe was a more unregenerate heathen than I was, but he was pretty bad."

This led them, all save Hodder, into comments on the character of the congregation the Sunday before, in the midst of which the rector was called away to the telephone. Sally Grover had promised to let him know whether or not they had found Kate Marcy, and his face was grave when he returned . . . . He was still preoccupied, an hour later, when Alison arose to go.

"But your carriage isn't here," said Phil, going to the window.

"Oh, I preferred to, walk," she told him, "it isn't far."

III

A blood-red October moon shed the fulness of its light on the silent houses, and the trees, still clinging to leaf, cast black shadows across the lawns and deserted streets. The very echoes of their footsteps on the pavement seemed to enhance the unreality of their surroundings: Some of the residences were already closed for the night, although the hour was not late, and the glow behind the blinds of the others was nullified by the radiancy from above. To Hodder, the sense of their isolation had never been more complete.

Alison, while repudiating the notion that an escort were needed in a neighbourhood of such propriety and peace, had not refused his offer to accompany her. And Hodder felt instinctively, as he took his place beside her, a sense of climax. This situation, like those of the past, was not of his own making. It was here; confronting him, and a certain inevitable intoxication at being once, more alone with her prevented him from forming any policy with which to deal with it. He might either trust himself, or else he might not. And as she said, the distance was not great. But he could not help wondering, during those first moments of silence, whether she comprehended the strength of the temptation to which she subjected him . . . .

The night was warm. She wore a coat, which was open, and from time to time he caught the gleam of the moonlight on the knotted pearls at her throat. Over her head she had flung, mantilla-like, a black lace scarf, the effect of which was, in the soft luminosity encircling her, to add to the quality of mystery never exhausted. If by acquiescing in his company she had owned to a tie between them, the lace shawl falling over the tails of her dark hair and framing in its folds her face, had somehow made her once more a stranger. Nor was it until she presently looked up into his face with a smile that this impression was, if not at once wholly dissipated, at least contradicted.

Her question, indeed, was intimate.

"Why did you come with me?"

"Why?" he repeated, taken aback.

"Yes. I'm sure you have something you wish to do, something which particularly worries you."

"No," he answered, appraising her intuition of him, "there is nothing I can do, to-night. A young woman in whom Mr. Bentley is interested, in whom I am interested, has disappeared. But we have taken all the steps possible towards finding her."

"It was nothing - more serious, then? That, of course, is serious enough. Nothing, I mean, directly affecting your prospects of remaining - where you are?"

"No," he answered. He rejoiced fiercely that she should have asked him. The question was not bold, but a natural resumption of the old footing "Not that I mean to imply," he added, returning her smile, "that those prospects' are in any way improved."

"Are they any worse?" she said.

"I see the bishop to-morrow. I have no idea what

position he will take. But even if he should decide not to recommend me for trial many difficult problems still remain to be solved."

"I know. It's fine," she continued, after a moment, "the way you are going ahead as if there were no question of your not remaining; and getting all those people into the church and influencing them as you did when they had come for all sorts of reasons. Do you remember, the first time I met you, I told you I could not think of you as a clergyman. I cannot now - less than ever."

"What do you think of me as?" he asked.

"I don't know," she considered. "You are unlike any person I have ever known. It is curious that I cannot now even think of St. John's as a church. You have transformed it into something that seems new. I'm afraid I can't describe what I mean, but you have opened it up, let in the fresh air, rid it of the musty and deadening atmosphere which I have always associated with churches. I wanted to see you, before I went away," she went on steadily, "and when Eleanor mentioned that you were coming to her house to-night, I asked her to invite me. Do you think me shameless?"

The emphasis of his gesture was sufficient. He could not trust himself to speak.

"Writing seemed so unsatisfactory, after what you had done for me, and I never can express myself in writing. I seem to congeal."

"After what I have done for you!" he exclaimed: "What can I have done?"

"You have done more than you know," she answered, in a low voice. "More, I think, than I know. How are such things to be measured, put into words? You have effected some change in me which defies analysis, a change of attitude, - to attempt to dogmatize it would ruin it. I prefer to leave it undefined - not even to call it an acquisition of faith. I have faith," she said, simply, "in what you have become, and which has made you dare, superbly, to cast everything away. . .It is that, more than anything you have said. What you are."

For the instant he lost control of himself.

"What you are," he replied. "Do you realize - can you ever realize what your faith in me has been to me?"

She appeared to ignore this.

"I did not mean to say that you have not made many things clear, which once were obscure, as I wrote you. You have convinced me that true belief, for instance, is the hardest thing in the world, the denial of practically all these people, who profess to believe, represent. The majority of them insist that humanity is not to be trusted. . ."

They had reached, in an incredibly brief time, the corner of Park Street.

"When are you leaving?" he asked, in a voice that sounded harsh in his own ears.

"Come!" she said gently, "I'm not going in yet, for a while."

The Park lay before them, an empty, garden filled with

checquered light and shadows under the moon. He followed her across the gravel, glistening with dew, past the statue of the mute statesman with arm upraised, into pastoral stretches - a delectable country which was theirs alone. He did not take it in, save as one expression of the breathing woman at his side. He was but partly conscious of a direction he had not chosen. His blood throbbed violently, and a feeling of actual physical faintness was upon him. He was being led, helplessly, all volition gone, and the very idea of resistance became chimerical . . . .

There was a seat under a tree, beside a still lake burnished by the moon. It seemed as though he could not bear the current of her touch, and yet the thought of its removal were less bearable . . . For she had put her own hand out, not shyly, but with a movement so fraught with grace, so natural that it was but the crowning bestowal.

"Alison!" he cried, "I can't ask it of you. I have no right - "

"You're not asking it," she answered. "It is I who am asking it."

"But I have no future - I may be an outcast to-morrow. I have nothing to offer you." He spoke more firmly now, more commandingly.

"Don't you see, dear, that it is just because your future as obscure that I can do this? You never would have done it, I know, - and I couldn't face that. Don't you understand that I am demanding the great sacrifice?"

"Sacrifice!" he repeated. His fingers turned, and closed

convulsively on hers.

"Yes, sacrifice," she said gently. "Isn't it the braver thing?"

Still he failed to catch her meaning.

"Braver," she explained, with her wonderful courage, "braver if I love you, if I need you, if I cannot do without you."

He took her in his arms, crushing her to him in his strength, in one ineffable brief moment finding her lips, inhaling the faint perfume of her smooth akin. Her lithe figure lay passively against him, in marvellous, unbelievable surrender.

"I see what you mean," he said, at length, "I should have been a coward. But I could not be sure that you loved me."

So near was her face that he could detect, even under the obscurity of the branches, a smile.

"And so I was reduced to this! I threw my pride to the winds," she whispered. "But I don't care. I was determined, selfishly, to take happiness."

"And to give it," he added, bending down to her. The supreme quality of its essence was still to be doubted, a bright star-dust which dazzled him, to evaporate before his waking eyes. And, try as he would, he could not realize to the full depth the boy of contact with a being whom, by discipline, he had trained his mind to look upon as the unattainable. They had spoken of the future, yet in these moments any consideration of it was blotted out. . . It was only by degrees that he collected himself sufficiently to be able to return to it. . . Alison took up the thread.

"Surely," she said, "sacrifice is useless unless it means something, unless it be a realization. It must be discriminating. And we should both of us have remained incomplete if we had not taken - this. You would always, I think, have been the one man for me, - but we should have lost touch." He felt her tremble. "And I needed you. I have needed you all my life - one in whom h might have absolute faith. That is my faith, of which I could not tell you awhile ago. Is it - sacrilegious?"

She looked up at him. He shook his head, thinking of his own. It seemed the very distillation of the divine. "All my life," she went on, "I have been waiting for the one who would risk everything. Oh, if you had faltered the least little bit, I don't know what I should have done. That would have destroyed what was left of me, put out, I think, the flickering fire that remained, instead of fanning it into flame. You cannot know how I watched you, how I prayed! I think it was prayer - I am sure it was. And it was because you did not falter, because you risked all, that you gained me. You have gained only what you yourself made, more than I ever was, more than I ever expected to be."

"Alison!" he remonstrated, "you mustn't say that."

She straightened up and gazed at him, taking one of his hands in her lithe fingers.

"Oh, but I must! It is the truth. I felt that you cared - women are surer in such matters than men. I must conceal nothing from you - nothing of my craftiness. Women are crafty, you know. And suppose you fail? Ah, I do not mean failure - you cannot fail, now. You have put yourself forever beyond failure. But what I mean is, suppose you were compelled to leave St. John's, and I came to you then as I have come now, and begged to take my place beside you? I was afraid to risk it. I was afraid you would not take me, even now, to-night. Do you realize how austere you are at times, how you have frightened me?"

"That I should ever have done that!" he said.

"When I looked at you in the pulpit you seemed so far from me, I could scarcely bear it. As if I had no share in you, as if you had already gone to a place beyond, where I could not go, where I never could. Oh, you will take me with you, now, - you won't leave me behind!"

To this cry every fibre of his soul responded. He had thought himself, in these minutes, to have known all feelings, all thrills, but now, as he gathered her to him again, he was to know still another, the most exquisite of all. That it was conferred upon him to give this woman protection, to shield and lift her, inspire her as she inspired him - this consciousness was the most exquisite of all, transcending all conception of the love of woman. And the very fulness of her was beyond him. A lifetime were insufficient to exhaust her . . . .

"I wanted to come to you now, John. I want to share your failure, if it comes - all your failures. Because they will be victories - don't you see? I have never been able to achieve that kind of victory - real victory, by myself. I have always succumbed, taken the baser, the easier thing." Her cheek was wet. "I wasn't strong enough, by myself, and I never knew the stronger one . . . .

"See what my trust in you has been! I knew that you would not refuse me in spite of the fact that the world may misunderstand, may sneer at your taking me. I knew that you were big enough even for that, when you understood it, coming from me. I wanted to be with you, now, that we might fight it out together."

"What have I done to deserve so priceless a thing?" he asked.

She smiled at him again, her lip trembling.

"Oh, I'm not priceless, I'm only real, I'm only human - human and tired. You are so strong, you can't know how tired. Have you any idea why I came out here, this summer? It was because I was desperate - because I had almost decided to marry some one else."

She felt him start.

"I was afraid of it;" he said.

"Were you? Did you think, did you wonder a little about me?" There was a vibrant note of triumph to which he reacted. She drew away from him. a little. "Perhaps, when you know how sordid my life has been, you won't want me."

"Is - Is that your faith, Alison?" he demanded. "God forbid! You have come to a man who also has confessions to make."

"Oh, I am glad. I want to know all of you - all, do you understand? That will bring us even closer together. And it was one thing I felt about you in the beginning, that day in the garden, that you had had much to conquer - more than most men. It was a part of your force and of your knowledge of life. You were not a sexless ascetic who preached a mere neutral goodness. Does that shock you?"

He smiled in turn.

"I went away from here, as I once told you, full of a high resolution not to trail the honour of my art - if ,I achieved art - in the dust. But I have not only trailed my art - I trailed myself. In New York I became contaminated, - the poison of the place, of the people with whom I came in contact, got into my blood. Little by little I yielded - I wanted so to succeed, to be able to confound those who had doubted and ridiculed me! I wasn't content to wait to deny myself for the ideal. Success was in the air. That was the poison, and I only began to realize it after it was too late.

"Please don't think I am asking pity - I feel that you must know. From the very first my success - which was really failure - began to come in the wrong way. As my father's daughter I could not be obscure. I was sought out, I was what was called picturesque, I suppose. The women petted me, although some of them hated me, and I had a fascination for a certain kind of men - the wrong kind. I began going to dinners, house parties, to recognize, that advantages came that way . . . . It seemed quite natural. It was what many others of my profession tried to do, and they envied me my opportunities.

"I ought to say, in justice to myself, that I was not in the least cynical about it. I believed I was clinging to the ideal of art, and that all I wanted was a chance. And the people I went with had the same characteristics, only intensified, as those I had known here. Of course I was actually no better than the women who were striving frivolously to get away from themselves, and the men who were fighting to get money. Only I didn't know it.

"Well, my chance came at last. I had done several little things, when an elderly man who is tremendously rich, whose name you would recognize if I mentioned it, gave me an order. For weeks, nearly every day, he came to my studio for tea, to talk over the plans. I was really unsophisticated then - but I can see now - well, that the garden was a secondary consideration . . . . And the fact that I did it for him gave me a standing I should not otherwise have had . . . . Oh, it is sickening to look back upon, to think what an idiot I was in how little I saw....

"That garden launched me, and I began to have more work than I could do. I was conscientious about it tried - tried to make every garden better than the last. But I was a young woman, unconventionally living alone, and by degrees the handicap of my sex was brought home to me. I did not feel the pressure at first, and then - I am ashamed to say - it had in it an element of excitement, a sense of power. The poison was at work. I was amused. I thought I could carry it through, that the world had advanced sufficiently for a woman to do anything if she only had the courage. And I believed I possessed a true broadness of view, and could impress it, so far as I was concerned, on others . . . .

"As I look back upon it all, I believe my reputation for coldness saved me, yet it was that very reputation which increased the pressure, and sometimes I was fairly driven into a corner. It seemed to madden somemen - and the disillusionments began to come. Of course it was my fault - I don't pretend to say it wasn't. There were many whom, instinctively, I was on my guard against, but some I thought really nice, whom I trusted, revealed a side I had not suspected. That was the terrible thing! And yet I held to my ideal, tattered as it was. . . "

Alison was silent a moment, still clinging to his hand, and when she spoke again it was with a tremor of agitation.

"It is hard, to tell you this, but I wish you to know. At last I met a man, comparatively young, who was making his own way in New York, achieving a reputation as a lawyer. Shall I tell you that I fell in love with him? He seemed to bring a new freshness into my life when I was beginning to feel the staleness of it. Not that I surrendered at once, but the reservations of which I was conscious at the first gradually disappeared - or rather I ignored them. He had charm, a magnificent self- confidence, but I think the liberality of the opinions he expressed, in regard to women, most appealed to me. I was weak on that side, and I have often wondered whether he knew it. I believed him incapable of a great refusal.

"He agreed, if I consented to marry him, that I should have my freedom - freedom to live in my own life and to carry on my profession. Fortunately, the engagement was never announced, never even suspected. One day he hinted that I should return to my father for a month or two before the wedding . . . . The manner in which he said it suddenly turned me cold. Oh," Alison exclaimed, "I was quite willing to go back, to pay my father a visit, as I had done nearly every year, but - how can I tell you? - he could not believe that I had definitely given up-my father's money . . . .

"I sat still and looked at him, I felt as if I were frozen, turned to stone. And after a long while, since I would not speak to him, he went out. . . Three months later he came back and said that I had misunderstood him, that he couldn't live without me. I sent him away....Only the other day he married Amy Grant, one of my friends . . . .

"Well, after that, I was tired - so tired! Everything seemed to go out of life. It wasn't that I loved him any longer, - all had been crushed. But the illusion was gone, and I saw myself as I was. And for the first time in my life I felt defenceless, helpless. I wanted refuge. Did you ever hear of Jennings Howe?"

"The architect?"

Alison nodded. "Of course you must have - he is so well known. He has been a widower for several years. He liked my work, saw its defects, and was always frank about them, and I designed a good many gardens in connection with his houses. He himself is above all things an artist, and he fell into the habit of coming to my studio and giving me friendly advice, in the nicest way. He seemed to understand that I was going through some sort of a crisis. He called it 'too much society.' And then, without any warning, he asked me to marry him.

"That is why I came out here - to think it over. I didn't love him, and I told him so, but I respected him.

"He never compromised in his art, and I have known him over and over to refuse houses because certain conditions were stipulated. To marry him was an acknowledgment of defeat. I realized that. But I had come to the extremity where I wanted peace - peace and protection. I wanted to put myself irrevocably beyond the old life, which simply could not have gone on, and I saw myself in the advancing years becoming tawdry and worn, losing little by little what I had gained at a price.

"So I came here - to reflect, to see, as it were, if I could find something left in me to take hold of, to build upon, to begin over again, perhaps, by going back to the old associations. I could think of no better place, and I knew that my father would, be going away after a few weeks, and that I should be lone, yet with an atmosphere back of me, - my old atmosphere. That was why I went to church the first Sunday, in order to feel more definitely that atmosphere, to summon up more completely the image of my mother. More and more, as the years have passed, I have thought of her in moments of trouble. I have recovered her as I never had hoped to do in Mr. Bentley. Isn't it strange," she exclaimed wonderingly, "that he should have come into both our lives, with such an influence, at this time?"

"And then I met you, talked to you that afternoon in the garden. Shall I make a complete confession? I wrote to Jennings Howe that very week that I could not marry him."

"You knew!" Hodder exclaimed: "You knew then?"

"Ah, I can't tell what I knew - or when. I knew, after I had seen you, that I couldn't marry him! Isn't that enough?"

He drew in his breath deeply.

"I should be less than a man if I refused to take you, Alison. And - no matter what happens, I can and will find some honest work to support you. But oh, my dear, when I think of it, the nobility and generosity of what you have done appalls me."

"No, no!" she protested, "you mustn't say that! I needed you more than you need me. And haven't we both discovered the world, and renounced it? I can at least go so far as to say that, with all my heart. And isn't marriage truer and higher when man and wife start with difficulties and problems to solve together? It is that thought that brings me the greatest joy, that I may be able to help you . . . . Didn't you need me, just a little?"

"Now that I have you, I am unable to think of the emptiness which might have been. You came to me, like Beatrice, when I had lost my way in the darkness of the wood. And like Beatrice, you showed me the path, and hell and heaven."

"Oh, you would have found the path without me. I cannot claim that. I saw from the first that you were destined to find it. And, unlike Beatrice, I too was lost, and it was you who lifted me up. You mustn't idealize me." . . . She stood up. "Come!" she said. He too stood, gazing at her, and she lifted her hands to his shoulders

. . . . They moved out from under the tree and walked for a while in silence across the dew-drenched grass, towards Park Street. The moon, which had ridden over a great space in the sky, hung red above the blackness of the forest to the west.

"Do you remember when we were here together, the day I met Mr. Bentley? And you never would have spoken!"

"How could I, Alison?" he asked.

"No, you couldn't. And yet - you would have let me go!"

He put his arm in hers, and drew her towards him.

"I must talk to your father," he said, "some day - soon. I ought to tell him - of our intentions. We cannot go on like this."

"No," she agreed, "I realize it. And I cannot stay, much longer, in Park Street. I must go back to New York, until you send for me, dear. And there are things I must do. Do you know, even though I antagonize him so - my father, I mean - even though he suspects and bitterly resents any interest in you, my affection for you, and that I have lingered because of you, I believe, in his way, he has liked to have me here."

"I can understand it," Hodder said.

"It's because you are bigger than I, although he has quarrelled with you so bitterly. I don't know what definite wrongs he has done to other persons. I don't wish to know. I don't ask you to tell me what passed between you that night. Once you said that you had an affection for him - that he was lonely. He is lonely. In these last weeks, in spite of his anger, I can see that he suffers terribly. It is a tragedy, because he will never give in."

"It is a tragedy." Hodder's tone was agitated.

"I wonder if he realizes a little" she began, and paused. "Now that Preston has come home - "

"Your brother?" Hodder exclaimed.

"Yes. I forgot to tell you. I don't know why he came," she faltered. "I suppose he has got into some new trouble. He seems changed. I can't describe it now, but I will tell you about it . . . . It's the first time we've all three been together since my mother died, for Preston wasn't back from college when I went to Paris to study . . . ."

They stood together on the pavement before the massive house, fraught with so many and varied associations for Hodder. And as he looked up at it, his eye involuntarily rested upon the windows of the boy's room where Eldon Parr had made his confession. Alison startled him by pronouncing his name, which came with such unaccustomed sweetness from her lips. You will write me to-morrow," she said, "after you have seen the bishop?"

"Yes, at once. You mustn't let it worry you."

"I feel as if I had cast off that kind of worry forever. It is only - the other worries from which we do not escape, from which we do not wish to escape."

With a wonderful smile she had dropped his hands and gone in at the entrance, when a sound made them turn, the humming of a motor. And even as they looked it swung into Park Street.

"It's a taxicab!" she said. As she spoke it drew up almost beside them, instead of turning in at the driveway, the door opened, and a man alighted.

"Preston!" Alison exclaimed.

He started, turning from the driver, whom he was about to pay. As for Hodder, he was not only undergoing a certain shock through the sudden contact, at such a moment, with Alison's brother: there was an additional shock that this was Alison's brother and Eldon Parr's son. Not that his appearance was shocking, although the well-clad, athletic figure was growing a trifle heavy, and the light from the side lamps of the car revealed dissipation in a still handsome face. The effect was a subtler one, not to be analyzed, and due to a multitude of preconceptions.

Alison came forward.

"This is Mr. Hodder, Preston," she said simply.

For a moment Preston continued to stare at the rector without speaking. Suddenly he put out his hand.

"Mr. Hodder, of St. John's?" he demanded.

"Yes," answered Hodder. His surprise deepened to perplexity at the warmth of the handclasp that followed.

A smile that brought back vividly to Hodder the sunny expression of the schoolboy in the picture lightened the features of the man.

"I'm very glad to see you," he said, in a tone that left no doubt of its genuine quality.

"Thank you," Hodder replied, meeting his eye with kindness, yet with a scrutiny that sought to penetrate the secret of an unexpected cordiality. "I, too, have hoped to see you."

Alison, who stood by wondering, felt a meaning behind the rector's words. She pressed his hand as he bade her, once more, good night.

"Won't you take my taxicab?" asked Preston. "It is going down town anyway."

"I think I'd better stick to the street cars," Hodder said. His refusal was not ungraceful, but firm. Preston did not insist.

In spite of the events of that evening, which he went over again and again as the midnight car carried him eastward, in spite of a new-born happiness the actuality of which was still difficult to grasp, Hodder was vaguely troubled when he thought of Preston Parr.

Choose from Thousands of 1stWorldLibrary Classics By

Ada Leverson
Adolphus William Ward
Aesop
Agatha Christie
Alexander Aaronsohn
Alexander Kielland
Alexandre Dumas
Alfred Gatty
Alfred Ollivant
Alice Duer Miller
Alice Turner Curtis
Alice Dunbar
Ambrose Bierce
Amelia E. Barr
Andrew Lang
Andrew McFarland Davis
Andy Adams
Anna Sewell
Annie Besant
Annie Hamilton Donnell
Annie Payson Call
Annonaymous
Anton Chekhov
Arnold Bennett
Arthur Conan Doyle
Arthur M. Winfield
Arthur Ransome
Atticus
B.H. Baden-Powell
B. M. Bower
Baroness Emmuska Orczy
Baroness Orczy
Basil King
Bayard Taylor
Ben Macomber
Bertha Muzzy Bower
Bjornstjerne Bjornson
Booth Tarkington
Boyd Cable
Bram Stoker
C. Collodi
C. E. Orr
C. M. Ingleby
Carolyn Wells
Catherine Parr Traill
Charles A. Eastman
Charles Dickens
Charles Dudley Warner
Charles Farrar Browne
Charles Ives
Charles Kingsley
Charles Klein
Charles Lathrop Pack
Charles Whibley
Charles Willing Beale
Charlotte M. Braeme
Charlotte M. Yonge
Charlotte Perkins Stetson
Clair W. Hayes
Clarence Day Jr.
Clarence E. Mulford
Clemence Housman
Confucius
Cornelis DeWitt Wilcox
Cyril Burleigh
D. H. Lawrence
Daniel Defoe
David Garnett
Don Carlos Janes
Donald Keyhoe
Dorothy Kilner
Dougan Clark
Douglas Fairbanks
E. Nesbit
E.P.Roe
E. Phillips Oppenheim
Edgar Rice Burroughs
Edith Van Dyne
Edith Wharton
Edward J. O'Biren
Edward S. Ellis
Edwin L. Arnold
Eleanor Atkins
Eliot Gregory
Elizabeth Gaskell
Elizabeth McCracken
Elizabeth Von Arnim
Ellem Key
Emerson Hough
Emily Dickinson
Enid Bagnold
Enilor Macartney Lane
Erasmus W. Jones
Ernie Howard Pie
Ethel Turner
Ethel Watts Mumford
Eugenie Foa
Eugene Wood
Evelyn Everett-green
Everard Cotes
F. H. Cheley
F. J. Cross
Federick Austin Ogg
Ferdinand Ossendowski
Francis Bacon
Francis Darwin
Frances Hodgson Burnett
Frances Parkinson Keyes
Frank Gee Patchin
Frank Harris
Frank Jewett Mather
Frank L. Packard
Frank V. Webster
Frederic Stewart Isham
Frederick Trevor Hill
Frederick Winslow Taylor
Friedrich Kerst
Friedrich Nietzsche
Fyodor Dostoyevsky
G.A. Henty
G.K. Chesterton
Gabrielle E. Jackson
Garrett P. Serviss
Gaston Leroux
George Ade
Geroge Bernard Shaw
George Durston
George Ebers
George Eliot
George MacDonald
George Meredith
George Orwell
George Tucker
George W. Cable
George Wharton James
Gertrude Atherton
Grace E. King
Grace Gallatin
Grant Allen
Guillermo A. Sherwell
Gulielma Zollinger
Gustav Flaubert
H. A. Cody
H. B. Irving
H.C. Bailey
H. G. Wells
H. H. Munro

H. Irving Hancock
H. Rider Haggard
H. W. C. Davis
Hamilton Wright Mabie
Hans Christian Andersen
Harold Avery
Harold McGrath
Harriet Beecher Stowe
Harry Houidini
Helent Hunt Jackson
Helen Nicolay
Hendrik Conscience
Hendy David Thoreau
Henri Barbusse
Henrik Ibsen
Henry Adams
Henry Ford
Henry Frost
Henry James
Henry Jones Ford
Henry Seton Merriman
Henry W Longfellow
Herbert A. Giles
Herbert N. Casson
Herman Hesse
Homer
Honore De Balzac
Horace Walpole
Horatio Alger Jr.
Howard Pyle
Howard R. Garis
Hugh Lofting
Hugh Walpole
Humphry Ward
Ian Maclaren
Inez Haynes Gillmore
Irving Bacheller
Israel Abrahams
Ivan Turgenev
J.G.Austin
J. Henri Fabre
J. M. Barrie
J. Macdonald Oxley
J. S. Fletcher
J. S. Knowles
J. Storer Clouston
Jack London
Jacob Abbott
James Allen
James Andrews
James Baldwin

James DeMille
James Joyce
James Lane Allen
James Lane Allen
James Oliver Curwood
James Oppenheim
James Otis
James R. Driscoll
Jane Austen
Jens Peter Jacobsen
Jerome K. Jerome
John Burroughs
John Cournos
John F. Kennedy
John Gay
John Glasworthy
John Habberton
John Joy Bell
John Kendrick Bangs
John Milton
John Philip Sousa
Jonas Lauritz Idemil Lie
Jonathan Swift
Joseph A. Altsheler
Joseph Carey
Joseph Conrad
Joseph E. Badger Jr
Joseph Hergesheimer
Joseph Jacobs
Julian Hawthrone
Julies Vernes
Justin Huntly McCarthy
Kakuzo Okakura
Kenneth Grahame
Kenneth McGaffey
Kate Langley Bosher
Kate Langley Bosher
Katherine Cecil Thurston
Katherine Stokes
L. A. Abbot
L. T. Meade
L. Frank Baum
Latta Griswold
Laura Lee Hope
Laurence Housman
Leo Tolstoy
Leonid Andreyev
Lewis Carroll
Lilian Bell
Lloyd Osbourne
Louis Tracy

Louisa May Alcott
Lucy Fitch Perkins
Lucy Maud Montgomery
Lydia Miller Middleton
Lyndon Orr
M. Corvus
M. H. Adams
Margaret E. Sangster
Margaret Vandercook
Margret Penrose
Maria Edgeworth
Maria Thompson Daviess
Mariano Azuela
Marion Polk Angellotti
Mark Overton
Mark Twain
Mary Austin
Mary Catherine Crowley
Mary Cole
Mary Hastings Bradley
Mary Roberts Rinehart
Mary Rowlandson
M. Wollstonecraft Shelley
Maud Lindsay
Max Beerbohm
Myra Kelly
Nathaniel Hawthrone
Nicolo Machiavelli
O. F. Walton
Oscar Wilde
Owen Johnson
P.G. Wodehouse
Paul and Mabel Thorne
Paul G. Tomlinson
Paul Severing
Percy Brebner
Peter B. Kyne
Plato
R. Derby Holmes
R. L. Stevenson
R. S. Ball
Rabindranath Tagore
Rahul Alvares
Ralph Henry Barbour
Ralph Waldo Emmerson
Rene Descartes
Rex Beach
Rex E. Beach
Richard Harding Davis
Richard Jefferies
Richard Le Gallienne

Robert Barr
Robert Frost
Robert Gordon Anderson
Robert L. Drake
Robert Lansing
Robert Lynd
Robert Michael Ballantyne
Robert W. Chambers
Rosa Nouchette Carey
Rudyard Kipling
Samuel B. Allison
Samuel Hopkins Adams
Sarah Bernhardt
Selma Lagerlof
Sherwood Anderson
Sigmund Freud
Standish O'Grady
Stanley Weyman
Stella Benson
Stephen Crane
Stewart Edward White
Stijn Streuvels
Swami Abhedananda
Swami Parmananda
T. S. Ackland
T. S. Arthur
The Princess Der Ling
Thomas A. Janvier
Thomas A Kempis
Thomas Anderton
Thomas Bailey Aldrich
Thomas Bulfinch
Thomas De Quincey
Thomas H. Huxley
Thomas Hardy
Thomas More
Thornton W. Burgess
U. S. Grant
Valentine Williams
Various Authors
Victor Appleton
Virginia Woolf
Walter Camp
Walter Scott
Washington Irving
Wilbur Lawton
Wilkie Collins
Willa Cather
Willard F. Baker
William Dean Howells
William le Queux
W. Makepeace Thackeray
William W. Walter
Winston Churchill
Yei Theodora Ozaki
Yogi Ramacharaka
Young E. Allison
Zane Grey

www.ingramcontent.com/pod-product-compliance
Lightning Source LLC
Chambersburg PA
CBHW020547310726
48979CB00008B/1120/J

9781421806952